Speculative North
Science Fiction, Fantasy, and Horror

Published by *TDotSpec Inc*

Speculative North Team

Lead Editor
David F. Shultz

Fiction Editor and Managing Editor
Don Miasek

Poetry Editor
A.M. Todd

Marketing & Operations
Mitchell "the itch" Harris

Social Media Lead
K. M. McKenzie

Submissions Editors

Anna P.L.
Vineet Bhalla
Brandon Butler
Jeff Butler
Wayne Cusack
Justin Dill
Mitchell Harris
Calder Hutchinson
Paul Jarvey
K. M. McKenzie

Don Miasek
Luc Moreau
Emil Terziev
Marty Hoefkes
Shivani Kamdar
Y.M. Pang
Jessica Rust
Marlaina Stocco
A.M. Todd

Publisher
TDotSpec Inc

Project Backers

Kickstarter Supporters

We would like to extend a huge thank you to all of our project backers, without whose generosity *Speculative North* would not have been possible.

A. M. Todd
Annelise Knoot
Barbara Campbell
Bart Vervaet
Bryan Dawe
Cat Girczyc
Catherine Oyiliagu
Dan Allen
Daniel Merritt
David Perlmutter
Ed Rockwell
Emil Pellim
Eric Jepson
EssentialEdits.ca
Ian Chung
Irena K.

J Kyle Kelsey
James Downe
Jeffrey R. Butler
Kim Lightle
Lawrence Marzari
Lisa Cai
Margret Treiber
Maria Haskins
Mark Carter
Marlaina Stocco
Martin Munks
Michael Luscombe
Michael Weckworth
Mike Rimar
Nancy Kay Clark

Natalie Garceau
Pauline Lim
Peter G. Reynolds
Peter Hargraves
Peter Vroomen
R. Graeme Cameron
Rahul Bhagat
Randal Heide
Rob Petrungaro
Scott Thrower
Sean W. Scully
Stephanie A.
Suzanne Barcza
Wendy L Schultz

Lifetime Subscribers

We would like to thank the following supporters, who believed in our mission enough to become life-time subscribers to *Speculative North*.

/amqueue
Ellen Michelle
Joshua Lee Cooper
Kumsal Obuz

Richard Ohnemus
Robbin Webb
Thomas Bull

Top Backer

A super-special thank you goes out to our top supporter, whose generous donation funded an entire issue of *Speculative North*!

Anthony Nijssen

Introduction to Inaugural Issue
David F. Shultz

Speculative North is a Canadian magazine dedicated to the celebration, promotion, and enjoyment of speculative literature in its various forms. Our mission is to foster a community of diverse voices in speculative literature, to create an enduring virtual space for readers and writers, and to promote the growth and flourishing of the speculative literature community. For our inaugural issue, I thought it was important to introduce the team behind *Speculative North*, to discuss our philosophy and methods for putting together the magazine, and to invite you to take part in this exciting new literary vista in the most important role of all —the reader. We hope to have readers as dedicated to and passionate about speculative fiction as we are. To that end, I'd like to talk about who we are, and some of the features of *Speculative North*.

The *Speculative North* Team
Speculative North is the joint product of volunteers from the *Toronto Science Fiction and Fantasy Writers,* the *Toronto Dark Fiction Writers,* and other unaffiliated volunteers, and is published by *TDotSpec Inc.* While the magazine is new, it was a long time

in the making, and comes from a thriving and established speculative fiction community residing mostly in Toronto. The *Toronto Dark Fiction Writers*, a group of over 200 members, has run regular writing meetings for over five years. The 660-member *Toronto Science Fiction and Fantasy* has as many as 240+ RSVPs in a month for its various writing-related events (all online as of the pandemic). *TDotSpec Inc* has produced six anthologies, and in its best month has distributed over 2500 units across its various titles; as of the publication of issue #1 of *Speculative North*, *TDotSpec Inc* has published 150 different authors, emerging and established, from across the world.

Previous TDotSpec titles

Anatomy of an Issue

In every issue of *Speculative North* we aim to include at least one story in each of the categories of science fiction, fantasy, and horror; at least one first-time-publication author; at least one Canadian author; at least one speculative poem; and at least three writers who self-identify as writing from a historically marginalized perspective.

Diversity is a strength and an asset in any community, but especially in writing communities, where human experience is both the primary subject and the raw material of creation. *Speculative North* seeks out a wide array of voices, experiences, and perspectives, because diversity enriches our stories, and it enriches our lives.

Non-Fiction Features

Speculative North supports the flourishing of speculative literature through showcasing its art and discussing its craft. Various non-fiction features engage the art of speculative literature through reviews, literary criticism, discussions of craft, and writing exercises.

The non-fiction features are intended for readers and writers alike, and we hope there is a large crossover between the two groups; all writers should also be readers, and all readers should try their hand at writing. For readers and writers, non-fiction discussion encourages appreciation for the craft and a deeper engagement with the art. For technical discussions and writing exercises, our goal is not just to promote development of current writers, but also to encourage readers to become writers themselves, and, we hope, submit their own story to *Speculative North*.

Editorial Process

At *Speculative North*, we're looking for original, compelling, and thought-provoking speculative fiction from wide array of voices and perspectives.

For our first open call for submissions, we received over 1.4 million words from writers around the world, each of which was read at least twice by volunteers from our reading team! Stories that made it to the shortlist were then read by a larger team of Submissions Editors, who voted on stories to provide a tentative lineup, and then debated the stories for inclusion at our editorial roundtable.

As part of our goal of supporting authors, we have maintained a 100% personalized response rate to submitting authors. This was possible thanks to our amazing team of volunteer readers, who worked hard to provide detailed and thoughtful comments on all submissions.

Speculative Fiction Defined

Speculative fiction has multiple definitions, but is commonly considered an umbrella term that encompasses science fiction, fantasy, and (speculative) horror. For our editorial purposes, we cast a wide net; we won't pass on an otherwise good story because it doesn't have enough magic or advanced technology.

Genre definitions are eternally in dispute. But broadly speaking, the essence of speculative literature is "world-building". These stories all take place in worlds that we recognize as apart from our own, because of the presence of some element that can only exist in the imagination, given what we know of our current reality—things that are magical or incompatible with our world, in the case of fantasy, or things that are beyond our technological capacity or empirical understanding, in the case of science fiction.

Speculative writers don't only create characters and conflict, settings and scenes—they create new worlds. Readers of speculative fiction don't only meet characters—they travel to alternate realities. Speculative fiction has all the strengths of non-speculative fiction, with the added power of imaginatively reinventing reality.

Funding and Distribution

Speculative North is produced and distributed on a not-for-profit model with the primary goal of supporting authors, by providing paid opportunities for publication, and by putting their stories in front of as many readers as possible.

The main cost in creating a magazine is time, and the team of volunteers behind *Speculative North* can't be thanked enough for the hard work and hours they put into the magazine. The next biggest cost is author payments, and other costs include cover image acquisition, printing and shipment for physical copies, and occasional minor costs like formatting and design work, currency exchange fees, and so on. The money for all this is provided primarily by crowd-funding backers, whose generosity makes it possible to produce the magazine.

People have varying ability to pay, and we don't believe that should limit their participation in literary culture; people shouldn't be priced out of reading stories. We are grateful for all of our readers, and would rather have many people reading the magazine for free than to have some people not read it because we've set an arbitrary price-point. Thankfully, because of the generosity of our crowdfunding supporters, we can distribute the magazine in various formats, some of which are free.

The PDF early-release format is provided first to backers and authors; the eBook (Kindle) and paperback formats are provided to backers who have chosen that option. After a delay, the eBook and paperback formats are made available for purchase on Amazon at a minimal cost. A month after release, the PDF format of the issue is made freely available to any interested reader through the TDotSpec website. We hope that this distribution model balances our goals of maximizing readership and raising enough funds to continue to support authors.

Final Note

Thank you so much for being a reader of *Speculative North*. This wouldn't be a community without readers like you. I hope you have as much fun reading the magazine as we had putting it together. I'm looking forward to many future issues, and I hope you will become a long-time reader of *Speculative North* and an active member of the literary community we are all building together!

—David F. Shultz

Contents

Kariku's Ocean
A. B. Eyers

I did not go to the funeral.

There were three ships leaving Kormorant that day, and I took the third—a former cruiseline refitted as slow streamer. None of the original furniture remained, but occasional stretches of hallway were still carpeted, floor to ceiling, with a thick but faded shag. It had been burgundy once, but around every other corner now was a muted ambush of mauve.

And there was the view screen.

It was on the rear of the ship. For the first three days (after which, with a tremendous clunking of engines, we hit our true stride and the stars dissolved into streamers) the wall of reinforced resin showed us our world, shrinking mist-green into a vast dark. There had once been padded benches facing the screen—you could see bolt holes in the floor—but the room was now a secondary hold, and boxes of dried kystrik buds were stacked nearly to the ceiling. We had to squeeze between the columns in order to see.

We squeezed between each other's grief, too. Someone was always crying, there. One boy—older than me, but with a soft face and large, wet eyes—did nothing *but* cry. He would sit with his back to the boxes, tears soaking the collar of his shirt, drinking and eating only what was put into his hands.

His grief was heavy, bruising, and I kept my distance.

This was my understanding:

The light that left from Kormorant a century ago is only reaching Jao now. That light is history. Memories. Moments drifting outward, lost to us but moving. Always moving. To explore space is to explore the past. The other passengers were running from their ghosts, their dead, their failures. Me? I was chasing mine. As that ship accelerated I thought maybe, if I went far enough, I could catch the light that had left from Kormorant before.

That was my understanding then.

•

I was born on Kormorant. (Green world. Mud world. Home of the whorl drive, planet where pain sleeps.) On the morning of my ninth birthday my father took me to the shipyards. We stood on the lower docks, swamp crabs clacking oversized pincers in chorus below us, and watched the skimmers take off. They tumbled from high platforms and climbed the air. At the bow of each balanced a single person, the long braid of a terrin driver slung over one shoulder, right foot hooked into the rudder line, hands ready in the nets. Some were coming in, heavy and low by the mudflats. They teemed with jewelled life, with hard shiny bodies.

I loved those skimmers.

"Every one of them," my father said, "is born in our factory. You remember the swarm we saw last week? How fast it went?"

It had been like nothing else. Liquid free-falling through the air, changing direction faster than I could follow. I nodded.

He pointed to a skimmer just taking off, the girl at its helm only a little older than me.

"Each of them has to go faster."

She wavered, then rose. Trembled in the wind.

"Everything must be in sync," my father said, following her rise. "Like a body. Better. But most important is the whorl drive. That's what keeps her airborn. If that clay cracks..." he spread his hands. The skimmer paused, hovered, then succumbed to gravity and dove.

"Two lessons today," said my father. "At the workshop I will teach you to turn the wheel that shapes the whorl drives."

The girl's right foot flicked back and forth, controlling sudden shifts in direction. She was laughing. It stole my breath.

"But also this. Remember this. Today," said my father, and the girl pulled up, and sunlight broke into pieces against her hull. She circled the shipyards once, twice, higher with each curve, braid pressed against her cheek. "I am putting her life in your hands," he told me. He rested a hand on my shoulder, and it should have been heavy. The weight of responsibility should have pinned me to the ground. Instead I hardly felt it. I was watching that airborn speck, and I felt light as laughing.

•

They call Jao 'The Isle of Light', but the first three months I spent there were in darkness. It was quiet, claustrophobic, cool, and dry. The clack and clutter of a hundred looms in the common cavern, the slick of silk against my thumbs, the smell of sulphur as the earth belched heat around us.

Isle of Light. It is a small, cold world whose people scrape a living from its frozen belly. If it weren't for the moths, and galactic demand for their silk, the radiated slag heap that is Jao would be abandoned. As it is, ships come only twice a year, exchange a cargo of uprooted humans for raw silk, and are gone.

Those first months we gathered cocoons, scraped them by feel from cave walls into great, soft sacks. It was summer, which meant radiation. Eleven hundred humans—indigenous and migrant workers together—followed the moth migration underground to wait out the sun. I was furious, and trapped.

And then, finally:

"Come out with us," he said.

I remember I stared.

I'd been sleeping. Outside my hammock, his face hung like a fish in the darkness, white and muscled. "What?"

He said it again, and his face came into focus, and I knew him. Mase. He was from Kormorant, a red-head from one of the early Polish settlements.

"Your family died," I said. My voice rasped. "I heard about the fire." The fish that was his face contorted—muscle spasms in the deep. "Who's 'us'?"

"Alele," he said. "You'll like her."

It was fall then, and the silk was no good. Cocoons dissolved into sticky messes when we touched them. I was tired of the caves.

I said, "Yes."

•

The people of Jao are fair—none of the warm browns of Kormorant (mud people of the mudflats). I thought of them as snow: yielding and insubstantial. They melted in the face of conflict, had no gods, no laws to speak of, few taboos. A passionless people.

Alele was one of them.

In the brighter lights of the communal cavern, her fair hair was a cloud. She and Mase had snowshoes—broad ovals of woven cane—tucked beneath their arms. "This is Balu," he told her. "He'll do better than me. He used to fish the mud flats back on Kormorant. The snow..." he turned to me. "It's impossible to walk on."

He sounded far too cheerful, but when I looked to see if Alele agreed, her face was blank. Soft. "Take these," she told me, and handed me a pair of snowshoes.

The upper levels of the caves of Jao stand empty through the summer. As we ascended it was so silent, so still, that I thought we were disturbing something sacred.

"It's like a spell," Mase whispered to me.

"Like we're breaking it," I replied.

I'd seen frost before, but nothing like this. It grew from the stone walls like a fleet of petrified wings, delicate and filigreed. It trembled with our passing.

We followed one long tunnel to where it switched back on itself, but when we made the last turn we stopped, struck dumb by the light.

I had once blistered the heel of my hand on a hot forge. The heat was so intense it hadn't feel like heat at all, only like pain. This light was like that. I staggered.

"It gets easier," Mase's voice said from just in front of me.

"Just squint." They were fastening the snowshoes onto their booted feet, and I did the same, fumbling with the laces. When it was done I stumbled after them, squinting ferociously. Out of the tunnel and into the white world of Jao. It blistered my mind.

I fell immediately.

The snow was soft. I'd thought the shoes would keep us on the surface, but they sank a little, tangled in each other, sent me pitching forward. I registered first only the blessed dimming of that light. But my feet were trapped. Mittens protected my hands and forearms, a heavy coat my torso, but snow worked its way into gaps by my wrists and neck, found bare skin and burned. I tried to wrench free and only worked myself deeper into the blue shadows.

Then hands were grasping me beneath the armpits, pulling me clear. Alele.

She did not laugh. "It takes practice," she said.

I thought of the mud flats, of the easy way I traversed them, snake-skin skis slick under my soles. I had no dignity here. Kariku would have laughed.

Kariku.

•

I was alone at the counter when the bell went, and I looked up to see the door closing behind her. Black braid looped twice and pinned, sharp green eyes, a lively mouth.

The girl from the docks.

She moved like she flew: like the carass beetles. Liquid black light.

"I saw you flying."

She stuck her chin in the air.

"I don't know what you're talking about, little brother."

I stared until the defiant chin came down and she giggled.

"Well fine. So did half the docks, anyway. They won't leave me alone with another skimmer for *weeks*."

My eyes widened. "Did you *steal* it?"

"Not exactly" She pulled a clay-baked beetle from her pocket, rolled it on the counter to crack the casing and tossed the meat into her mouth, leaned on one elbow and grinned. "I'm an apprentice, but I'm not approved for solo flights."

But how...?" Skimmers were suicide without proper training.

The girl just smiled. "I flew my brother's all last year after he went to bed, and nobody ever knew."

I was awed. "I'm Balu," I said.

"Kariku,"

"One day I'll make you a skimmer," I told her.

She didn't laugh.

I'd learn later that Kariku laughed at everyone. But at the nine year old boy propped behind a too-tall counter, promising the world, she only nodded. Like it was her due. Like she understood what that gift would mean from me.

"If you do," she said, "I'll take you up."

The door swung open and my brother Lem stood in the frame, aloof and too clean—he never set foot in the workshop. "Bal," he said, "you're needed."

I rolled my eyes at Kariku, but she was watching Lem with the same tilt to her head I'd seen when she chased the carass beetles. As I slumped into the workshop I could hear them talking, her voice suddenly deeper, clearer. Laughing.

•

I blinked against the memory and the sunlight alike, struggled after my companions—the only splashes of colour I could see. We shuffled single-file into the wind as my snowshoes tripped me up. Snow melted down my collar. The light pried open cracks in my mind, poured into them.

My friendship with Kariku, after that first meeting, set like a dislocated shoulder, slotted into place like it belonged. Kariku and I would meet on my rooftop after dusk, her with a handkerchief of beetles, me with dried strips of sour mash. We'd spit carapaces into the night.

Then, "Let's go to the mud flats!" she'd say, and swing down from the roof. Kariku always went hand-under-hand, half falling down the drainpipe, legs akimbo. "Come on!" she'd crow up at me.

And I always did, clinging shamefully to the wall.

We'd tied a length of cord to the docks and kayaked a short distance into the winding, changeable waterways, careful, careful. The air had been sweet with sun-baked leaves.

I collided with Mase. Alele, ahead of us, dropped her mittens and raised the dart gun to her mouth.

"Some people use nets," Mase whispered. "You can stun a whole flock with one net. This is the old way."

She fired, and the snow erupted into motion, then was still. We moved forward. Alele reached it first and held the body up. It was a bird. So white it seemed blue, except where blood speckled its beak. Even its eyelids were feathered. I wanted to touch them.

After that I began to lose focus. Pain settled into a concentrated knot behind my eyes. To soothe my dry mouth I plucked frost crystals from the surface of the snow, melted them on my tongue. It was the strangest feeling, those sharp edges slipping into liquid.

Alele walked beside me for a while, though the trail was too narrow. "Mase says there is no hunting on your world," she said.

I thought of the skimmers, the way they stalked the swarms, ambushed and chased them.

"Not like this," I said. "There's nothing this big."

"You eat beetles? Just little beetles?"

Was she laughing at us? I couldn't tell.

"You would die on our world," I told her. I imagining her squat body trying to navigate the flats and snorted.

•

By the time my brother left for university in the capital, Kariku was a gawky thirteen, as close to awkward as someone with her grace could get, all her desire focused on Lem. I was beginning to mind.

That was the year my father showed me how to skin a stone snake by splitting the hide along its back, keeping the slick belly intact. "Here," he told me. He put the knife down and draped the empty skin over his hand like a scarf. There was blood on his wrist. "Slide your hand along it. Feel how you don't feel anything."

I was rapt. Machines were one thing, but I wanted to learn the old ways too, how to make a skimmer with my own hands, blood on my wrists.

He'd built his first skimmer as a courting gift for my mother. When she retired it, he stripped the snakeskin from its boards and built a bed. After she died—the way terrin drivers do, a meteoric crash into the mud flats—he still slept there.

It took the better part of a month to make my first pair of snakeskin skis, but I made Kariku's in just two weeks.

It was a new kind of freedom. The waterways for trade between hilltowns were well known to us by then, for all that they shifted with the rains. Any fool could kayak them, with a little care. The flats themselves, navigable only by ski, were choked with keffer roots, thick and horribly dangerous. Apart from stone snakes and the mud itself (it drowned several people a year) the flats housed hoards of tstse flies and leeches, and many of the trees harboured a parasitic slime that burned unprotected skin. We were often warned of getting lost, of the mists that could descend and stay for weeks.

We didn't care.

I can still see Kariku, a ferocious burn on the back of her neck, gliding through a loop of roots ahead of me, squinting up through the branches, always up.

We found pools of clear water deep in the flats, fished in them for eels. We ate the soft, unfamiliar flesh in the crooks of trees, skis dangling from our feet. Those eels were the largest animals on Kormorant; the abundance of protein made us sick.

•

When the darkness came, it was full of noises. Small guttural mutters. My neck prickled.

"Ke-luck," the voices said. "Ke-luck-ke-luck"

Alele was at my elbow. "It means 'go back,'" she said. "They say it when the night falls." She handed me the blow gun and clapped her hands together. A flock of birds took flight around us, their wing-beats like a frightened heart. "Ke-luck-ke-luck-ke-luck!" went the cacophony.

"They *speak*?" I asked.

She looked at me, inscrutable beneath her hood.

"It scared me too," Mase said. "But they're not... not intelligent. People made a word out of their sound, but it doesn't *mean* anything."

But it horrified me, as we walked back towards the caves. That quiet chuckling from the darkness.

Just before the door I picked a piece of frost, had it on my tongue before I realized something was different. It was soft, soft, muted, and it thrashed against the roof of my mouth.

Reflexively I swallowed, feelinginsect legs on the back of my tongue. I must have made a noise, because Mase turned to look at me. As if on cue the whole patch of frost—the whole fleet of silk moths—took to the air, refracting the sunset, indistinguishable from the frost. Such perfect camouflage.

It was dim in the tunnel. My head felt skewered, my eyes like dirt had been rubbed into them. At the second turn I stopped, braced my back against the stone wall, slid to rest my head on my knees.

Alele was beside me. Too close.

"You are sun-touched," she said. She touched my cheek. The silk oils had softened my hands in just a season—hers were hardly there. Like a feather. Like a moth's wing on my tongue. I flinched.

"Rest," she said.

By the time I reached my hammock—supported by Mase—I was in agony, and nearly blind. Alele came to us sometime later, brought me an oily dark soup that I did not eat.

•

My brother was gone for three years, and I didn't miss him. Fifteen isn't twelve, after all. By fifteen I'd started to admire the sensuality of Kariku's body as well as its grace. Did they talk about us, in the hilltown? Our hours alone together, how we'd return dirty and smiling from the flats? I wanted them to talk.

I thought she'd forgotten Lem.

He was eighteen when he came home. There was a handfasting that weekend, and I watched Kariku pull him onto the dance floor, fierce eyes fixed flashing on his. I watched her pull him into the shadows by our house.

My innocent friend.

I followed them, but Kariku didn't need rescuing. Lem was the innocent.

"Are you sure?" he asked.

Her laughter was delighted, sure.

Everything changed. Lem had planned only a short visit, but it stretched on, and on, till the whole hilltown *did* talk. It was Krishikira, the harvest time that comes once every six years; the mudflats were bursting with green, the kystrik trees in bud. Our workshop was in high gear turning out skis and kayaks instead of skimmers. The resinous buds of the kystrik trees are prized throughout the galaxy. They are our main export, and the reason Kormorant was settled at all.

On the first day of harvest, Kariku joined our family. When it came time to pair up she sidled over to me, smiling at Lem.

"You're no match for Balu on the flats," she told him. "Don't miss me too much."

It was like old times. The two of us moved easily between kayak and skis, working grove-by-grove. She was in the final stage of her apprenticeship now, and was learning to process the carass beetles, so she wore the metal exoskeleton—ceremonial and useful—that made a claw of her left hand. It was useful for kystrik leaves too, she told me. We filled sack after sack.

But when we turned to go home, fog came down, shrouding the waterways. We drifted, each with a hand on the other's kayak, calling intermittently into the growing darkness and hearing no answer, until we bumped into a small hillock—mostly mud, but some true soil—and without speaking climbed onto it. I had a flint and steel in my pocket, and we set to building a fire, the smoke aromatic in our faces. I was numb with fear.

"Here," Kariku said, and held something to my lips. I opened my mouth before I realized that what she held was a kystrik leaf.

It was sharply astringent, and after only a moment I shoved it into my cheek. Kariku chewed solemnly, and she went to her kayak and took out her kerchief of beetles. We made a mud oven like we had as children.

I could feel myself calming as the night sharpened around us. I was deeply relaxed, but prickled with awareness. I could smell the fire, the beetles, Kariku's skin. Her metal hand flashed, cracking carapaces for the sweet nutty meat. Swamp crabs scuffled up from the water and ringed our fire. Her hair was black as the water. She looked a creature of steel and speed and fire.

"This is how my ancestors ate," she told me, grinning. She sat in the storyteller's pose, half-mocking. "When we first came to Kormorant, our provisions spoiled in the monsoon season and we starved. Many were the deaths. Some ate stone snakes and died of the poison, others ate swamp crabs and died of the madness. Others ate weeds and kystrik leaves and wasted away. But Kiku, the mother-of-us-all who was then a young girl, had a dream that the swamp crabs led her to food, and the next morning she watched them and learned to crack the carass beetle."

Her hands flashed in the darkness.

"And all were fed, but we save the wings for Kiva."

The tiny crabs crowded at our feet. In the firelight it seemed they worshipped there, small claws raised to her large one. I whispered the final line with her.

"*We save the dead for Kiva.*"

In that place, in the light of that fire, it felt like the invocation it was.

She raised a set of wings to throw to her audience and the light caught them. Made bold by the kystrik I reached out, touched them. My head was dancing.

"Your eyes are this colour," I said. "Just exactly this."

She scowled, flipped the wings to the crabs, who clacked a competition among themselves.

"Like a dead bug's wing?"

Just exactly like. I groped for a better answer.

"Or a kystrik leaf!"

It was true. The glossy green was deep and secretive enough, but it lacked her flash.

She laughed.

"Are my eyes so edible, little brother?" she held another leaf to my lips.

"I'm not your little brother," I said.

I meant it to sound dashing. It came out petulant. But things were in motion now. I picked up a kystrik leaf and held it towards her. She took it with her teeth.

"I don't want to be your little brother," I said.

Her eyes met mine. Our smoke floated low over the water.

Then Kariku reached up her hand and touched my cheek. Her fingers were cold, hard. Her hair swung down like the night and her face was full of fire.

"Balu, you're so young," she said. She was always saying that. "You'll forget me. I want you to forget me."

She drew away but I reached up, pressed her hand to my cheek, and her face... it opened. She was looking past my shoulder, and the light from someone's lantern fell across us. The magic broke. Kariku was smudged with soot, her eyes unfocused from the kystrik juice, her hair tangled.

She stood and ran to the water, clay grey on her calves, to my brother's kayak. The mist had cleared. I could see all too plainly as Kariku threw herself into Lem's arms. Other boats hung back, the people in them laughing. I saw Lem's eyes go to the open bag of kystrik leaves, to the discarded carapaces dulled by the fire, and then to me.

He grinned. He whispered something to Kariku.

My face was wet. I touched it, took my fingers away smudged with blood from where I'd pressed her claw to my cheek. The cut was deep.

•

It was Mase who found me in my hammock, spoke to me gently, and brought me food and drink. I'd been there some time.

"This is no way to live," he said, pressing a dried bean cake into my hand. "It's not even living, really." The stubble on his face was dark red. His skin looked roughened. Mase sighed, broke a piece of the cake, held it to my nose. The smell—dusty, wholesome—did its work. My hand came up of its own accord, and I ate.

"I don't want to live," I told him.

"Eat now," he said. "Live later."

I chewed, swallowed. He handed me a mug of something hot, and I drank.

"We built her skimmer," I said. "My brother and I." Then, "He was her lover. Kariku's."

It had been Lem's idea. "My money," he'd said, "your skills. The end of your apprenticeship, the end of hers... it's perfect timing."

Which is what I'd thought for years, although my fantasy had never involved his money. But I hadn't been able to resist.

Kariku liked a longer mast, a shorter rudder. She liked flexibility and speed—agility over stability. The safest skimmers are dangerous to fly, and the one we built her was a graceful death trap.

I knew she'd love it.

We carved the hull together.

"We weren't close," I told Mase. "But he worked hard. He was humble."

Some tasks he'd left to me. He stood watching as I fitted the whorl drive. Ran his hands endlessly over the snakeskin, but stood back as I fixed it in place.

"It was the closest we ever were," I said.

Mase crumbled me another cake. I let him do it.

"Did she crash?" he asked.

"No," I said. "She was perfect."

The bean cakes tasted like dust.

•

"Balu," she had said. I was turning the wheel in our workshop. Easily, now, after nine years. The trick was to never let it stop. She put her hand on mine, slowed the motion.

"Balu, I'm going up tonight."

She looked at me. Not the look of a sister. It made me pause, and in that pause I felt a hairline fracture start, then snap beneath my hands.

"I promised I'd take you, didn't I?"

I wanted to say, "I thought you forgot." I wanted to say, "Why now?" I wanted to ask what this meant to her. But I was already nodding.

I met her on the docks.

She was waiting on the upper dock, of course. When I

reached the platform she held her hand out, strong brown palm upturned, hauled me the last few feet.

The skimmer rocked in the wind, nudged us with excitement. Kariku patted the keel.

"You've got to leave everything on the ground," she said. "That's what they tell you before your first flight. Anger is too heavy to fly. So is love." It was like a challenge, the way she said it, but she didn't meet my eyes.

We climbed aboard. I was cramped in the hull, knees pressed to my chest. I felt like a child, just as unsettled by this girl as I always had been.

She launched us.

I've flown since. I've seen Kormorant shrink to nothing, felt gravity lose its grip. I have moved between worlds. That was nothing compared to this. We flew like we'd trained our whole lives for it. A swarm of carass beetles passed our flank and Kariku turned and kept pace, riding an invisible current. The beetles were black and green around us, flashing, and I could hear the clockwork music of their wings. I reached out, touched a bright body for one heartbeat, and then we were gone, diving hard and fast, her laughter bright in my ears. We didn't chase the light—we rode it.

I don't think I breathed in that skimmer. Maybe I haven't since.

Afterwards I felt like I'd learned the secret of escaping gravity, like my feet stayed planted only from politeness. Kariku was solemn. I saw on her face, that this had been the christening flight. That she'd been afraid and now was not.

"Balu," she said. She took my face between her hands, between her rough, strong hands, and I felt small. She always made me feel so small. Now, I thought, she would say it. She would take the unspoken thing between us, take it glittering between her fingers, and crack its hard shell and nourish us with its sweetness. She would make it spoken. Make it real.

She said, "Can I tell you something?"

I couldn't move. I felt the net scars rough on her palms. I said, "You shouldn't have taken me up. Your first ride should have been alone..."

She said, "I am going to handfast with Lem."

•

Mase was still watching me. Not caring how rude it was, I spat the last of my bean cake onto the stone floor, stood up.

"It doesn't matter," I told him. "She's dead."

•

She avoided me after that night, slid out of my life as easily as she'd once slid in, left no tracks.

Until my brother came to the shop.

"Yes?" I wiped my hands. Looked at him like he was just another customer. "Is there another major project you'd like me to undertake for free?"

He was quiet a long time. At last he said, "I'd like to talk to you, Balu."

"So? You're talking."

"About Kiku."

I shook my head.

"I don't know what happened," he continued. "And I don't understand your friendship. But I know her."

I must have scoffed.

"I do. And this can't go on. We need..."

And then she came in. Her lips were tight when she saw us frozen and guilty. She didn't speak, but when she turned on her heel Lem followed her, and did not come back.

I heard their voices late into that night, like water lapping at the bottom of the floorboards in monsoon season. Insistent. Monotonous. Going nowhere. They had fought many times before, the educated man and the young terrin driver, but never like this, never for so long and so furiously.

It was late when she left. I heard the tread of her feet in the hall, and then she paused by my door. We breathed in silence, separated by a scant inch of wood, listening.

"Balu?"

She scratched at the door, our secret childhood signal. Three quick, two long.

"Are you awake?"

I didn't answer.

"I'm going up," she said.

There was a tremor in her voice that had to be laughter; she never cried. She was laughing at me, I thought.

"I'd welcome a friend tonight," she said.

I lay there, hated her.

After some time I heard her leave, but not by the front door that led to the docks. I instead heard the door to the waterway open. Once as a child she had walked the ledge by that door nimble-quick and had slipped through my window. I thought she might do that now. I perfected the cold expression with which I would greet her. Perhaps she would be cold, would come to my bed...

I fell asleep waiting.

When I woke it was suddenly, with a dreadful foreboding.

It was morning, and light, and far too quiet.

My father and brother were gone. I walked the empty house in bare feet, too paralyzed with fear to go to the docks, to the market, to the workshop.

It was evening when they returned, kayaks slow in the water. My brother was out first. He passed me at the doorway with only a glance, but it spoke all. The weight of his grief capsized me.

I looked down from the porch to the water.

They were towing her kayak.

She lay atop it. Her hair was wet, loose around her shoulders. Her face was bloated and huge, and her slender hands were not sharp metal claws but curled human ones, and I thought two things in that second.

I thought of what she'd told me. That love is too heavy to fly.

I thought of the agony by which the stone snake kills.

And then I was drowning, and I thought no more.

The following morning I was gone.

•

Mase and Alele wouldn't let me starve. It was quiet in the caverns —more and more people were moving onto the surface. There was no work to be done, and we had all been paid—a small fortune by my standards back home. It wouldn't be long before the ships began to leave.

"Home or onwards?" I asked Mase one day.

"Neither," he said. He and Alele smiled simultaneously. I stood up as he continued, "Alele and me..."

"Good for you," I said. I turned away so I wouldn't see him take her hand. I made for my hammock. But Alele followed me. I stopped in one of the more open tunnels, where I could hear the thrum and clatter of the weavers, waited for her to speak. Her eyes were washed blue.

"We burn our dead," she told me.

It wasn't what I expected. I rocked back on my heels. On Kormorant only the bodies of murderers are burned. It is a ceremony visible for miles. On the day Mase's family died, hilltowns everywhere saw the smoke and assumed a different kind of tragedy.

"That's barbaric," I said.

She shrugged. "I took Mase to the grieving place. Where we etch their names into the rock. He did so. Many do. It, for him, was healing."

My body was tense with the desire to be away from her.

"I know it is not the same. But Kar—"

Almost I hit her. She stopped, her eyes frank, calm.

Kariku at the center of this cold moon, her temper smoothed by snow and feathers? No. She wasn't here. I'd left Kormorant to find her, but she'd been too fast for me.

"Let her rest," the girl said.

Why? So I could live my life as if she hadn't lived?

Kariku. The sharp cut on my cheek from her touch, the funeral I did not go to, where the crabs consumed her body.

Kariku.

I walked away.

I took the next ship home.

At the back of my mind was the thought that to find Kariku's trail I would have to go back, but it was more than that, and less. With Alele I had felt for the first time the magnitude of what I had done, what I had left behind.

I couldn't have mourned with Mase, but my brother... I'd seen my grief on Lem's face. If there was comfort to be found it was there.

But I'd left.

Time moves differently aboard a streamer. It stretches out across the bedsheets, snoozes there while on the planets things rush on like always. I was eighteen, maybe. When we landed, Lem would be eighty.

The other passengers were migrant workers, coming to pick the kystrik leaves. They had no attachment to Kormorant. And so I spent much of my time alone at the view-screens, looking forward into the darkness; looking back to the place I'd left.

When the green planet rose unchanged before us, we descended.

Grebe, Kormorant's third largest hilltown, had not changed since I left, or not much. I slept a heavy, troubled sleep by the shipyards, set off in the morning for my old home. But out on the flats, the years showed. Only the deepest waterways were more than a trickle now, and when I neared our hilltown I could see that the flats had receded from its base, leaving a wide stretch of sand. The hill itself was different too, lush with some new kind of greenery. Crops at last on Kormorant. No more sour mash, I hoped. I walked along the sand. Closer to home the changes were worse. Our workshop was derelict. Our house... it stood on stilts as it always had, but instead of mud surrounding it there was earth. Grass. I climbed the ladder, knocked. My mother opened the door.

"Come in, you fool," she said.

She was not my mother. My mother was dead. Had been dead even before I left. This woman was taller, rounder, but the expression on her face as it passed from rushed annoyance to confusion to shock, was one I remembered. She sat down suddenly on a seat by the door, her eyes fixed on me. We stared for a long moment. When she opened her mouth it was to shout, "Taja!" without taking her eyes from me.

After a moment another woman appeared in the low kitchen doorway. She was tall as well, with a nurturing, soft look. She frowned first at the other woman, then at me.

"What..."

The first said, "He just knocked at the door."

"So?"

"Well, look at him."

She did, long and hard.

"Who is he?" the first asked.

"He's..." Taja looked at me. "You'd better come inside," she said.

The house seemed smaller. Not because I had grown but

because there were more people in it. Another woman joined us, and a young man nearing adulthood. Each was silenced by the sight of me. For my part I was too wretched at the sight of them to speak. At last a girl entered. She was quick and dark, and she took in the circle of stares in an instant. She said to me, "Kiri knows who you are, but you must be one of us. Whose bastard are you?"

No one shushed her.

I shook my head miserably. "I'm Balu," I said. They were my brother's family, I could see that. He had married. The first woman clapped a hand to her mouth.

"I'm your uncle Balu," I told her.

There was a confused silence.

"I've been away," I said, trying not to cry. "On Jao."

The young man leaned forward. "In the silk caverns?" he asked. "I've always..."

But Taja spoke over him. "You'll want to see Father," she said. "I don't know how you knew to come."

I shook my head.

"He's..." she looked at her sisters. "He's dying."

And that was not a shock, not really.

He was very ill, Taja told me outside his room. His children, "Myself and Gat and Iche you've met, but you've two nephews as well, in town, and all the grandchildren have been in and out!" were there with him in what they thought to be his final days. His wife was dead. She looked at me carefully there. "She would have known the most about you," she said. "My mother knew everything."

I was glad she was dead. She could not have been like Kariku—not with daughters as graceless and foolish as these. Any one of them would topple a skimmer as soon as look at it.

"Are there still skimmers?" I asked abruptly.

She nodded, surprised. "Of course," she said. "The soybean crop doesn't do *that* well. We incubate swarms indoors now, but some families still train their children to fly." Her tone told me what she thought of this. "He's very poorly now," she said, nodding at my brother's door. "He may not... well. It'll do him good to see you, but he gets confused."

She paused.

"Stay here tonight," she said. "For however long. This is still your home if you want it."

She took her hand away.

"Don't answer now," she said. And then she left.

I stared at my brother's door. Already I wished I had not come.

But the door.

I opened it.

The old man sat upright in bed, propped by pillows, and my brother had never looked so at peace.

"Come in," he said. "Close the draft. Where's my tea?"

I shook my head, helpless.

"What's the use in all these offspring if they won't bring an old man his tea?" He laughed. "If your mother was alive!"

My mother was not alive.

"Well. No tea. What, then? More questions?" He peered at me. "Who *is* your mother?" he asked. "Taja?"

I shook my head.

"No. You'll have to excuse my memory. Iche, then?"

"I want to ask about Kariku," I interrupted.

He nodded slowly.

"I want to know what she said to you before she died," I said. "I want to know if she was going to leave you."

I hadn't meant to ask that. I'd thought we'd mourn together, that he could tell me—with the wisdom of all his years—how to honour her. But here he was, surrounded by his new family, no longer even mourning Kariku's *replacement...*

"Tell me," I said. And I heard the break in my own voice, the hairline crack that expanded, sent me spinning downward...

I clenched my fists and fought the tears.

When I looked up the old man was watching me, and for a second I saw my brother in his face.

It was as I had seen him once before, in the firelight behind Kariku, his eyes darting between my bloodstained cheek and her claw. It was a look of startled recognition, and of pity. When I saw it first it said, "I can't give you what you want."

It said the same thing now.

And then it was gone. "You'll have to ask your mother," the old man said. "I have trouble with my memory these days."

I was shaking. His breath was shallow, strained. I spoke into the sound of that breathing.

"You forgot her."

Nothing on his face but confusion.

"You never deserved her," I told him.

And then I turned. Fled.

•

Lem died that night.

It was beautiful: all fourteen of his grandchildren filled that house, crying and laughing and holding each other. It was hideous: stinking pus came up from his throat and had to be sponged off of his tongue. He'd always been so clean. When he choked we could smell it thick in the air, and we gagged with him, in sympathy and horror.

When it was over I slipped out, walked along what had been a waterway but was now sand. Tzetzes landed on my skin, sipped at the moisture there.

"You could stay."

My grand-niece. Her eyes the wide silvery grey of the mud flats under the moons. The way they used to look.

We began to walk.

"You lost someone before."

I nodded.

"That's why you left."

I nodded again.

And then, in front of this girl I would never know, I sat suddenly on the damp sand and began to cry.

She sat beside me, leaned her head up so the moons caught in her eyes, waited.

"But she isn't here," I said. "She isn't anywhere."

And I was drowning, drowning. The ocean of space not only above but around us, timeless and vast and forever, and I was drowning in it.

"I've never lost anyone," she was saying, tears in her eyes too.

"Not until now. But if this girl is anywhere, she's with you. Only with you, really...the world's moved on. Just like it will now, I guess."

How small her world was.

Then, like an afterthought, but meaning it, she said, "I'm sorry for you."

We sat a while longer, under the moons. When I could breathe again we stood, walked further. We made our way up the hill towards the workshop. The big sliding doors were the same, but they were stiff. The two of us put our backs into it, pushed them open.

In so many ways just the same.

We wandered through the machinery, touching pieces of it. The girl asked questions sometimes, and sometimes I answered them. We made our way to the centre, to the great wheel. It was intact. I put a hand to it but it was stuck. I felt again the depth of my grief, but now, with my hand on the wheel, this one thing that should never cease moving, I knew. I new what I had to do.

"She's with you," the girl had said.

I hadn't chased Kariku's light away from Kormorant; I'd carried it.

They'd all told me to accept it, to let her go, to get on with my life. But my brother was weak. Mase was weak.

I wouldn't be weak.

I would go on.

I turned to my grand-niece. She was smaller than me, but her face was turned up, and in the dim light of the workshop I saw how pretty she was. More than that I saw that her face was always upturned, that she was another who looked always up, always out. There was something in her smile. Her eyes like somebody else's ocean.

She didn't need to be told. At the end of that long moment she smiled again, a little mockingly, and said, "Remember me out there, cousin."

But I don't think I ever knew her name.

•

I didn't go to the funeral.

Only one ship was leaving from Kormorant that day and I am on it now. We are going far, to the furthest edge of the known worlds. To Kaios, where the mariners say fire ants the size of stone snakes carve liquid pathways through the land, and the trees burn like pyres in the boiling earth.

When we reach it she will have been dead for three hundred of Kormorant's years.

I thought once that if I travelled far enough, fast enough, if I threw myself as recklessly into the void as she once did, I would reach her somehow, catch her light. I know now that there isn't any light. I look through the view-screens of this ship and there is only darkness, and I carry her through it.

From Kaios they say the exploration ships still leave. Less often now, but still they make their stately way into the unknown. Into the black. I'll go on. Five hundred years? A thousand? I'll pass through time untouched.

Until this world ends, until the star of our planet burns itself into oblivion and there are no more clay pits or kystrik leaves, or carass beetles, their wings the iridescent colour of a dead girl's eyes. I will bear her memory into eternity.

I will ride the ocean of my grief forever, and she will never be forgotten.

Author's Note:

I started writing this story in the winter of 2014, while on a two-month snowshoeing trip through the Yukon's Ogilvie Mountains. We had experienced unseasonably warm weather for a few days, and the snow was becoming increasingly soupy and awful. One morning we woke up to find that the temperature had dropped to -20 C, and because of the humidity and the sudden cold air, every surface for miles around was covered in the most incredible hoar frost. It looked as though a fleet of ice moths had landed all around us. We travelled for two days before a snowfall erased that frost. It remains one of the most beautiful things I've ever seen, and because of the remoteness of those mountains, we were the only people in the world who were seeing it. I couldn't get the image out of my head, and so I invented a moon to house it.

Tokyo Burning
Nathan Batchelor

The Master Poisoner ran through the halls of Edo Castle. She was careful not to touch her face where the giant snail's spit had splattered, careful not to let the screams of the panicked and dying break her composure.

The snails had descended from the sky on spindles of thin material, landing on the docks of Tokyo. The size of British cannons, the speed of Spanish horses, they chased and massacred the citizens. The Master Poisoner had fled from the teahouse, the assassination mission she was on a far thought in her mind. There was chaos and death all around as the snails belched corrosive spit. Fat and flesh hissed and boiled.

She slid the plank of wood through the latches of the door to the alchemist's lab. It smelled worse in the lab than outside, burnt fur and formaldehyde. There was a dog flayed open on a slab of metal. There were shelves and shelves of carelessly labeled vials. The soul of water. Tree's breath. The cough of a horse. None of the names made any sense to the Master Poisoner, despite her training in one of the best labs in the world on the stormy shores of Britain. And when she resorted to unstopping and smelling them, she found nothing that would kill the throbbing ache that razored across her face.

A scream went up somewhere in the castle. This floor. This hallway. The hiss of a snail's spit like the tide against the rocks. Her time was running out.

She quickly removed her kimono, the silk still smoking from the spit. She wore trousers beneath, feeling naked without the familiar wool against her legs. She slid underneath the table where the dog lay. Perhaps the snail would barrel through the door and kill her before she had time to pull the kaiken from her belt loop or down the poison intended for the man she had sailed to Japan to kill, the Black Beetle.

In her flight from the teahouse, she'd seen civilians scatter, racing toward the shelter of Buddhist temples or flinging themselves into the Tokyo Bay. She'd watched monks ringing the temple bells even as the snails ascended the walls with frightening speed. She had turned toward Edo castle, thinking the fortifications, moats, and soldiers there could offer more protection than a temple of pacifists.

But the enemy had downed the castle walls without a problem. And the soldiers? If there were any in the courtyard or barracks, she hadn't seen them.

The door rattled. The latch bowed.

"Hello. Is anyone inside? Please, the courtyard's crawling with them. The throne room and the barracks are burning," someone said.

A girl's voice? And why were things burning? The enemy hadn't seemed capable of starting fires. The Master Poisoner's head reeled with pain.

She threw off the latch, kaiken in her hand, ready for

whatever new hell waited behind the door. It was a boy in military garb. Not a Japanese, Dutch, or British uniform as she would have expected. But Russian. And so fresh off the heels of the war that had rocked Japan the year before in 1905.

His arm was severed at the elbow. The sleeve of his uniform hung in rags. Snail acid had cauterized the flesh shut around the bone, better than any British surgeon could do with boiling oil.

He spoke in breathless, broken Japanese. Loud enough to coax tings from jars. Loud enough to attract snails? The Master Poisoner didn't know by which sense they hunted.

She made motions with her hands. She pulled him close, whispered to him with her cobwebbed voice. Nothing but a throaty rasp.

The boy said in English, "Bloody hell, you're deaf. Bloody hell, we're going to die."

She slapped her hand over his mouth. "Not deaf. Mute," she signed.

·

Her father, the samurai, used to take his daughter up the steps of the castle. Where she'd stalk the halls, stealing looks at the other samurai, swords on their hips, feet so quiet as they moved like ghosts through the halls.

She could be a ghost. She could make no noise. She could kill, too, as she'd killed her mother during her birth. Something her father never mentioned but hung heavy in the Master Poisoner's mind. But the time of women samurai, the *onna-bugeisha*, had died out before she had been born, as the first bullets were fired across a battlefield.

Through her father's connections, she'd taken the opportunity to study on the other side of the world, where her skill in the lab, and doubtless her ethnicity, made the higher ups decide there was a certain type of work that would suit her.

When the first snail had landed, she was holding a vial of poison over a teapot in a crowded teahouse. She had been an hour late to the teahouse where the Black Beetle was to take tea in a meeting with local businessmen. All because of a chance mix-up on her ship. Her luggage was nearly lost, the poison with it.

The first snail had crashed through the top of the teahouse. Yakuzu had swarmed, pulling guns and swords from business suits and kimonos.

The snail sprayed a torrent of its black death. She watched a man melt like a candle, nothing left but bone, jewelry, a sword still sheathed. A drop of the acid splashed on her cheek, singeing the flesh away.

Men were running, scrambling. She knew the Black Beetle was somewhere among them. She had caught a flash of the tattoo, the scarab legs that wrapped around his ears, his scalp almost entirely inked over.

After the screams and the snail moved out of the teahouse, she stumbled into the streets. Tokyo, the city of her youth, had changed so much. She stared at the path she thought was to her old home. More screams rose above the water against the docks. A Geisha house toppled as a snail crashed through the walls. Women flooded out, white faces, skirts hiked above their knees. The snail followed, mowing them down with acid.

She turned away from home and ran for the castle.

•

There was an ink bin and brush beside the dead dog. She grabbed crinkly paper and struggled with the brush as she wrote. She had grown so used to using a quill.

"The Master Poisoner. Some name," the boy scoffed. "Why can't you speak?"

"Born mute. Now sit. You're hurt," she wrote. Then, "Your name?"

"Geoff." He moaned.

"I'm going to help you, Geoff. But you must be quiet."

She scanned the shelves, browsing the potions. This was a lab for the dead, not the living. Still, this lab should have what she needed. She just had to find it.

Geoff had an English accent. But he knew Japanese, and he wore a Russian uniform. He must be a spy, she thought.

Her heartbeat quickened when she found a vial labeled *Laudanum*. But when she smelled it, she knew it was only the base alcohol. She still needed opium.

She went through the boxes, turned over corpses of dogs wrapped in paper. Squids dried like jerky. She opened and smelled every unlabeled jar. Caught sight of her face in mirrored glass. Finally, she saw the damage the saliva had done to her face. Bone shone through her cheek.

She opened a box hidden beneath a tarp of rice paper. Opium, pure and white, bagged for smoking, not for laudanum. Still, it would work. She heated the burner, watched the solution bubble, and pressed the warm drink to Geoff's lips. A slow smile spread across his face. She took only a sip. A shot of bliss closed around her like a fist.

Clack. Clack. Clack.

There was the unmistakable sound of a snail somewhere close. She had to think fast. She had to move quietly. She grabbed a vial of sodium crystals and poured a circle around the door, quietly. If it was a snail, this would keep it away, right?

She felt like a fool. This wasn't a British garden. She didn't need a box of salt. She needed a rifle. She touched the vial of poison on her hip. Would her poison kill it? Perhaps if she heated the poison, the fumes would kill all three of them. The idea was tempting, but she was not ready to die.

There was the sound of a snail belching. The wooden door hissed. A steaming clop of wood fell to the floor. An eyestalk poked through.

Geoff's head lolled from the laudanum. "Is that you, Mama?"

She snuffed out the candles that lit the room with her fingers and backed into the corner where Geoff lay between shelves. The smell of his lavender soap sent her spiraling back to British cliffs, placing her hands carefully on jagged stones as she descended to the water. How she wished she were home.

Perhaps the snail wouldn't find them in the dark. Perhaps it relied on sight.

Geoff yelled, "I see you looking at me, girl. I've got a big surprise—"

The Master Poisoner slapped her hand over his mouth. But the damage was done. She could hear it moving, the awful screech as the legs of the table slid across stone.

She dared not move. The kaiken felt so small in her hand as the snail towered over them, swinging eyestalks in search of prey. A slice to the jaws, or a thrust in the eyestalk would maybe buy her time for an escape.

The face of the thing curled, swiveled, faster than it had any right to. She didn't know what was happening. Then the top half of the snail slid, separating from its body. The body slouched and steamed. The head fell to the ground at her feet.

The sound of a match in the dark. A woman in samurai garb, hair grey and pulled tight in a ponytail standing behind the snail. Cigarette dangling from her mouth. The woman lit the lamps with her cigarette. Wiped the mustard blood of the snail off her sword.

"Are you the Master Poisoner?" the samurai said, signing with her hands.

The Master Poisoner nodded.

"The Black Beetle sent me to get you."

•

Outside Edo Castle, on the same steps she'd stood on as a girl, she watched snails coming down in the evening sky. Countryside houses exploded like puffball mushrooms underfoot as they landed.

She had led Geoff drunkenly through the halls, the courtyard, stepping over bones, avoiding pools of saliva that boiled and hissed as flies and cicadas dipped and died inside. The samurai checked every hovel and inspected every citizen's remains. She was looking for something or someone.

"The Black Beetle has a ship prepared," the samurai said,

between sips of water from a waterskin. "Docked and leaving when we arrive. We can make it easily without interruptions. Through the forest."

She pointed to a patch of bamboo woods that separated the castle from the port. It was the only place the Master Poisoner had not seen a snail land, a black sea of bamboo surrounded by islands of fire.

The samurai smashed her cigarette underfoot. "But first we kill the traitor." Her sword was at the back of Geoff's neck before the Master Poisoner had time to react.

"He's a child," the Master Poisoner signed. Perhaps saving the boy had warmed her to him. Perhaps in this strange country, he was her link to that faraway island of clouds and cold that she thought of as home.

"He's in league with the demons," the samurai said. "Why would you, an assassin, care for the death of some foreigner boy? The isle of Britain has made you weak."

Geoff lulled on the steep. The Poisoner put her kaiken to the samurai's throat.

"Britain has only sharpened the blade that I am," the Master Poisoner signed. "Would you like to know how sharp?"

"The Black Beetle is wrong about you. I told him as much," the samurai said, sheathing her sword.

"A lot of people have been wrong about me," the Master poisoner signed.

"Butterflies?" Geoff said, examining a piece of ash on his hand like a jeweler. "Here, all the way in Bangkok?"

•

The rice fields were flooded. The water came up past the Master Poisoner's knee. She was careful to keep the vial of laudanum above the water. Geoff had grown afraid as he sobered. Not of the snails, but of the samurai who called herself Yuki. They were almost to the bamboo forest.

"You can't see where we're going. It's too dark," Geoff said.

"You'd rather I leave you here for the snails," Yuki said.

"You can. They trust me."

"Trust you enough to eat your arm off? Some friends they are."

The Master Poisoner picked up that Yuki was a warrior who'd fought in the Japanese-Russian war, who came home to a different country, one who didn't want her. No one, that is, but the Yakuza. Grudgingly, she sat for the needlepoint tattoos, abandoned her poems for dice. She'd learned to sign from the Black Beetle himself. The only thing keeping her from plunging a sword in her own belly was a son, an aide to the emperor. If that's who she looked for in the castle, the Master Poisoner didn't know. But with the carelessness Yuki swung her blade, the Master Poisoner wondered if Yuki had found what remained of her son in the courtyard.

Geoff wasn't sure what he was doing here. A Brit posing as a Russian. His troop was to be given a tour around the castle. While other British troops dressed as Russians toured granaries, paper-making factories, silk warehouses at the same time. The Master Poisoner knew what was going on. But she wasn't going to tell him that he'd been sent here to die in a Russian uniform.

Did that mean her home, Britain, was responsible for these

snails? Her thoughts were too clouded by the flood waters that rose above waist, fatigue, and the fight for survival. She couldn't make sense of anything.

There was a glimmer of hope against the tree line. A dozen soldiers lit by the glow of the blazes atop the flamethrowers they carried, backs bulging from the fuel tanks on their back. The fires made sense now. The Japanese soldiers had found something that would stop the creatures.

She splashed in the water, making as much noise as she could. Yuki's hand closed tightly on her wrist. The samurai made the signs for "shut up" and "run." Then she was running, legs churning against the water. Away from the soldiers.

They ran past farmhouses, traveling shrines untouched or razed to ash by fire. Water gave way to mud, gave way to rock, gave way to an unflooded spring. She ducked inside a grotto. Her legs burned. Her face burned. Her lungs ached. Dim firelight fled through cracks in the grotto's ceiling. Just enough to illuminate Yuki's face. The samurai motioned for them to be quiet. Geoff quivered in fear. Whimpered in pain.

Yuki signed "snail" then "man."

The Master Poisoner shook her head.

Then "man," "demon," "come," and "sky."

She barely had time to put the ideas together before she heard the footsteps outside in the water. Then the sound of snails.

Clack. Clack. Clack.

There was no exit to the grotto. They were cornered. By what? Men who looked like slugs? Slugs that looked like men? The Master Poisoner drew her kaiken.

Their faces appeared in the light of their flamethrowers. Featureless below the helmets, except for a spherical mouth, lined with long and thin teeth. Eyestalks that peaked from below helmets. Russian uniforms.

Yuki signed to her. "Run through them." Yuki's eyes told the story. She had found what remained of her son in the keep. "To the harbor. He's waiting."

The Master Poisoner grabbed Geoff, but he jerked away, letting loose a moan.

She pressed the remaining laudanum to Geoff's lips, feeling the pain ease out of him. He slumped to the ground. Yuki ran towards the slugmen. The Master Poisoner followed. Yuki's blade sounded in the night. Then her screams. The Master Poisoner broke through the bodies and never looked back.

•

She couldn't feel anything as she crashed into the water headfirst. If she had been burned by the slugmen or if adrenaline had wiped everything away, she didn't know. Into the woods, where she ran for what felt like forever. Finally, up a hill where the bamboo thinned. She came to a small house that overlooked the harbor, a rock garden, and a nude part of the ground where someone had meditated. A samurai's home. She went inside and collapsed on the floor.

It was night and raining when she woke. She cursed herself for sleeping. She stripped away her clothes, the wool trousers. Though the wool had burned through in places, her skin was untouched, except for a patch of singed hairs on her arm. She dressed herself in the ill-fitting man's garb she found in the house.

She did not realize how hungry she was until she saw the bowl of cold rice on the counter and the vegetables picked perhaps this morning resting on the small counter. She warmed food by the fire and ate until her belly swelled. She sat at the western style table and poured tea. She flipped through the poetry left out on the table. There was a feeling of safety that she couldn't place. Part of her thought she should stay. Part of her thought she should accept her fate here, forget the Black Beetle, the slugmen, the giant snails, watch the world burn. But another part, wanted to watch the Black Beetle writhe as the poison seized him, wanted to go home.

She was rubbing her finger around her cup when she bumped the table, the top sliding away to reveal more papers. Spy documents. Whoever lived here was working with the Yakuza. There were ink paintings of slugmen bowing before wigged and powdered British officials. The mention of their love for fire, and their reverence for the human form.

The documents referred to the slugmen and snails as the Hood. There were signed agreements for a war alliance between the Hood and the British, against another unnamed faction. It was soon apparent that the third faction was Japan. That Britain had caved to the Hood's wishes to watch a land burn, had supplied them with the flamethrowers. There were mentions of the Black Beetle, inventory records of Japanese tea leaves and gunpowder. From the documents, she could not figure out why the Black Beetle was the target of her assassination.

She smelled burning paper. When she looked up from them, she saw the walls igniting. In seconds, the house lit up like a paper lantern.

A troop of slugmen must have followed her into the forest. She didn't have much time to think. She burst through the paper wall at the back of the house, popping the stopper of the poison she carried in the vial.

The slugman nearest her let out a click of excitement or alarm. As his head jerked back to call, she splattered the poison over his face. Her attention cost her. Her foot caught on the root of a tree.

She tumbled down the top of the hill and landed on a terrace. She looked up to find a gravestone. The inscription read "Kuri." It couldn't be. That was her father's name. Had this been his home? No. He'd died months ago. That's when she'd received the letter and the kaiken she now wore on her hip. A traitor was living here, someone with the veneer of a samurai and the heart of a Yakuza.

She rolled and stared up into the eyeless face of a slugman. She hadn't noticed the cut across his face before. Yuri's sword must have done that. She watched his finger press the trigger. She smelled the fuel. She waited to die. But death did not come.

The slugman dropped his gun. His flesh swelled like a balloon. There was a sound like a train whistle as the body exploded. The poison had worked. She did not wait for the other slugmen to appear. She turned and scrambled down the hill, before hitting mud, slipping, the wind going out of her. She rolled. Down. Down. Down. Until she landed at the base of the hill, pain flooding her entire body.

When she looked up, she could see the lights of ships in the distance through the trees. Despite everything, a tinge of excitement rolled down her spine. The Black Beetle was on that ship and she had a vial of poison with his name on it.

•

She hacked away the last of the bamboo and saw the burning harbor before her. Her ankle was broken from the fall. She'd bound it with bamboo the way her father had shown her, stumbled gingerly through the forest toward the lights, the sounds of the Tokyo Bay. She fingered the vial in her pocket.

These Tokyo streets were familiar even in the darkness. The fish market, where Chang the Chinaman cut finer fillets than anyone in the city, the alleyway where she used to hide in the mornings, watching vegetable sellers push their carts to the town center. A footstep in some of the first concrete poured in Tokyo, her own footprint on this town. Still there. That recess filled with rain and ash as the city burned.

Noises swelled around her. Yakuza firing machine guns, swinging swords against the Hood. The clacking of slugmen, the sound of the large snails belching, and above it all, the ship's horn singing a siren's call.

She moved silently from shadow to shadow. She knelt in an alley, behind a charred and smoldering cart. A cat squatted smugly near her feet. In front of the pier, between her and the ship, a group of slugmen leaned over the smoldering husk of a man. They moved away, except for one, who squatted and took off his helmet. His feelers swayed in the wind.

The cat around her feet hissed and darted further down the alley. The slugman's eyestalks swung toward the alley. How odd his walk seemed as he came toward her, like a drunken man or a child who'd just gained command over their steps.

She did not move, hoping he would not see her. But he was more perceptive than she gave him credit for. Before she had time to grab her kaiken, he dove at her, knocking her from her squat.

She was not strong, but neither was the slugman. They rolled in the alley, fighting for position. She grabbed for her dagger but could not reach it. Instead she found the vial.

The slugman's call clacked loud enough to ring her ears. Boxes and baskets fell as they fought. She knew there would be more soon. She would have to use the poison on the slugman. She would have to find another way to kill the Black Beetle. The slugman's mouth opened, long lines of filaments in a circle that took up his whole face. She emptied the vial into his maw.

She waited for the swelling, the explosion of his flesh. Nothing.

He rolled her over, topped her, pressed a hand into the wound on her cheek. She screamed. Not from pain but from victory. She had found her kaiken, shoved the blade up into the maw. She prayed the blade struck home at something in its alien physiology. The liver, the intestine, the heart. It must have hit something. The slugman's body jerked and slumped atop her.

She could hear the other slugmen and snails. She ran. The rain was coming down sideways. The ocean churned and sloshed against the pier. Behind her the docks crawled with the Hood, a swarm of false faces and pseudopods.

A man was calling to her from the ship. She could barely see him on the ladder over the side of the battleship. Her balance swiveled. She was falling. But the man's hand caught her, pulling her up on the ship.

Machine guns clanged as men on the ship pelted the creatures on the pier. American business suits, tattoos bursting from sleeves and collars. Yakuza. She watched the snails and slugmen expand and explode.

"You are the Master Poisoner?" The man said.

She nodded.

"Finally. We've got her, lads," he said. "The Black Beetle has been waiting for you. Yes, he's cloistered himself below deck worrying."

The man led her to the captain's chamber. There were potted plants lined along the walls. The smell was overwhelming. Tea leaves like the ones she'd boiled in the samurai's house. A surgeon or some kind of doctor sat her down, dressed the wound on her face.

"What is all this?" she signed to the man who had led her here.

"You'll have to ask the Black Beetle," he said. "We run a tight-lipped operation. Wait here."

"Tell me how you got here," a voice said from the shadows.

She signed everything she could remember.

"A house in the woods with your father's grave?" He asked. "It was some chance you came across that, or perhaps no chance at all."

"You are the Black Beetle?" she signed.

"Yes," he said.

Her hand found the kaiken on her belt.

There was a reason the Hood had avoided the forest, he told her. The tea leaves her father had harvested in his forest house were their weakness, could kill them the way salt kills a garden slug. On the ship, they had been mixing gunpowder with the ground tea leaves.

"That's why he worked with the Yakuza," he said.

"I don't believe it," she signed. "My father would sooner have died than work with them."

"Everything happened very fast. And our government was prepared to turn its back on the people," the Black Beetle said. "They gave up the country for dead. But the Yakuza remained. The samurai were faced with a choice: join the Yakuza or watch their country burn."

That's why the castle had been empty, she thought. The residents had already fled, knowing what was coming.

"Father's hand was forced," she signed.

"Yes. Our spies found out rather quickly there were plants the Hood abhorred, teas they wouldn't touch when offered. We lost many men in Britain in the last year discovering which plants worked best against them. It was fate that our best weapon was a plant grown in the forest where your father lived."

It made sense now, why the slugman had exploded atop the hill. Why the one in the streets hadn't. It had nothing to do with her poison. The slugmen atop the hill had been exposed to the fumes of the tea she had boiled. Pure chance had saved her.

"They sent me to kill you," she signed. She didn't see much use in hiding anymore. "I aim to do it."

"And turn your back on your home?"

"Britain is my home."

"Still, you would do such a thing? Allow a force to destroy your true homeland? I don't believe it. I did not raise such a daughter, Uta."

Her name, the one she'd almost forgotten.

"I'm only sorry I couldn't be with you sooner," he said. "There is much red tape now. Even this, holding the ship for so long."

The Black Beetle stepped out of the darkness. She recognized the tattoo that enveloped his head. She would have recognized him regardless of the new tattoos, the shaved head. Her father. He wrapped his arms around her.

"I told them you hadn't died," he said. "I told them to wait."

In his arms, she felt the hate go out of her like a sickness.

"I should never have come," she signed. "I nearly killed you in the teahouse."

"No. I'm glad you came back. Our spies knew you were coming. I am only sorry this charade had to last so long. The Hood arrived before I was to reveal myself. Your poison was useless. It was replaced in your luggage mix-up."

She felt like a foolish little girl again.

The man came in and smiled when he saw them hugging. "Still set for Russia, Beetle?"

"Yes. We'll need allies for what awaits us," the Black Beetle said. He turned to Uta. "We can find you a boat in Korea if you'd still like to go back to Britain."

She shook her head. She was home. More home than she'd been in a long time.

It's Always Ice Time in the D.H.L.

Gregg Chamberlain

A bunch of the boys were boozing it up over at St. Peter's down the road a bit from Heaven's Gate. They knocked the first round over well before noon. It was now long past eight.

St. Peter was the Original Netminder, though not with a rod and reel. On Earth he and his mates made their living the hard way, casting nets night and day until the Lord offered them a much better deal. Now rock-solid as any heavenly foundation stone, it sort of made sense that when he got tired of greeting new arrivals to Paradise, good ol' Pete would set up shop with a little fisherman's grill on a site near the Pearly Gates. That it just happened also to be directly over Toronto with an angel's-eye view of the Gardens below in ol' Hogtown, well, just call it divine luck and let it go at that. Quite naturally every rink rat that found himself kicked upstairs sooner or later made himself at home at Pete's Place.

But on this one particular day it was anything but smiles and good cheer as the boys slugged down their beer. Doom and gloom filled the room and grew thicker all afternoon until you could dull your skates just by stepping inside. It had been that way since Valentine's Day and by Black Wednesday the heart that wasn't broke at St. Pete's by the impossible come true was made of stone for sure.

There would be no Stanley Cup, at least not for this year's crew. Down on Earth it would seem that not even the Great One or Super Mario together could salvage the dream.

Foster Hewitt sat grim-faced and silent at a table over in a corner. A single tear did a slow slide down his cheek as he listened to the T.V. hung up 'cross the room and the CBC sports announcer sounding the death knell.

"No one shoots and no one scores as Hockey Night in Canada is finally, officially cancelled for the rest of this year."

Not a single eye in the room was dry, though no one would admit to a tear. Lord Stanley's Cup would sit on the shelf. There'd be no parades this year.

Michael and a couple other angels quietly moved among the tables, emptying ashtrays, setting down glasses, and collecting empties. There were a lot of those.

Behind the bar, dressed in a black-and-white-striped referee's shirt and with his hair tied back in a pony tail, Jesus polished glasses. No surprise that he's at St. Pete's. After all, didn't he suffer the hardest cross-check of them all?

Jesus listened and nodded in sympathy as he filled up a clean mug with pure water and handed it over the bar to Maurice Richard. The Rocket, he drained the glass, not even noticing that it was now filled with the best beer that he'd ever tasted, and went on with his grumbling.

"I played when I was injured. This arm," he held it up for

Jesus to see, "I hurt once while moving furniture one weekend. Then they call that day, my day off, but they still call me to play. 'We need you, Maurice,' they say, and, me, I go. And I scored the goals even. Me! With my bum arm, and we won, we did, we beat those Leafs. We showed them Montreal is always better than Toronto, even when we hurt."

His lips twisted as if the beer had gone bad in his mouth and Richard began to mutter about "les maudits cochons" who had killed his beloved NHL. But he stopped when gentle-voiced Jesus raised a finger and said "Du calme, mon p'tit, du calme."

Then the Rocket, he relaxed and nodded his head. He held out his glass for another refill instead. Over at a side table Horton dismally flicked timbits with a finger between a goal made of two upright beer bottles, never missing and not caring. Number 50 whizzed through just as Turk Broda boomed into the room, stumped over to the bar and dropped himself down onto an empty stool that groaned a bit loudly at the weight.

"Well, I asked," Turk said aloud for all to hear. "But the Horsemen said no, though Death, he abstained. Said he didn't want to take sides, at least that's what he claimed. Famine muttered about meal breaks and Plague said he felt kinda low. War said he might consider saddling up if it was the Superbowl. But not a one was eager to ride for the Cup."

Heads shook all around then slowly hung down, though whether to curse or pray was hard to say. If the atmosphere in the room was full of gloom before it was downright mournful now.

The Stanley Cup not even worth an Apocalypse? It really was the end of the world. Or at least it would have been if Some

People could get their priorities straight.

Just when it seemed that spirits could not sink any lower or things get any much worse, into St. Peter's walked Satan, which prompted at least one surprised curse.

Now Don Cherry is known as a sharp-dressed man, it is true, but most times it is still proper to give the Devil his due. Although far better known as a world-champion liar, Ol' Scratch could give even "Grapes" tips on fashionable attire.

Yes, the Prince of Darkness is the one who really puts the s.t.y.l.e. in the word "style". Which explains a fair bit all the puzzled looks directed his way as he clumped across the room towards the bar. For the Ol' Gentleman was bundled up in a bulky skidoo suit, fiery red, of course, with clunky snow boots, and a bright-red balaclava-style tuque pulled down over his pointed ears.

Astonished silence was soon replaced with growled mutterings and murmurings.

"What's he doing here?"

"Come to gloat, maybe."

"Yeah, that's right, he probably saw it coming."

"Probably the one who did it."

"Yeah."

"Yeah!"

"YEAH!"

Without a sign that he'd heard even one solitary word, the Devil stopped at the bar and signed for a beer. Jesus poured water from the tap and handed it over to his not-so-better half. Satan accepted the mug and took a long, slow pull at the amber nectar it now contained. Swallowed. Licked his lips. Nodded thanks to the Lord.

Then he turned around and gave the whole room one long, slow look. There was a sudden pause. But everyone still looked ready to drop gloves and charge if given just cause.

Satan brought up his hands as if he held up a stick to block a check to the head. "I know what you're thinking but it's not true," he said. "Believe it or not but I had nothing to do with what's happed to Our Game. I'm as surprised as any of you and that's the—" he hesitated, then sighed, "—that's the God's honest truth."

Everyone waited. But no thunderbolt crashed through the ceiling to smite ol' Nick where he stood. Behind the bar Jesus continued polishing glasses and wiping a rag over the wood.

Satan dropped his tuque on the bar, unzipped his skidoo suit and peeled it down to his hips. Underneath he had on a Devils uniform shirt covered with player signatures from the '03 finals when Jersey and Anaheim bashed away at each other.

"It's true," the Devil said again to every disbelieving face. "I'm as disappointed as anyone else with the way the NHL's put the season into the deep-freeze. Hockey has always been my favourite Canadian sport, a pretty decent way to spend a Saturday night in winter."

A voice sang out from the back. "Thought I read somewhere that you were a curling fan!"

There were a few chuckles at that. But the Devil, he frowned and took a long look around, then spat into a butt-filled bucket of sand by the bar. "Curling," he sneered. "Too much of a gentleman's game for me. Too friendly, too polite, too—"

"Canadian?" offered Jesus with a quiet smile as he handed his adversary another beer.

Satan rolled an eye at the quip but made no reply as he wiped foam off a lip.

"Hockey has always done a nice bit of business for me," he explained, "running through da—, uh," —here ol' Lucifer caught a severe look from behind the bar—"uh, darn near every one of the major sins, starting from Pride and Arrogance among the hometown fans and players all the way through to Rage and Hate when the fights break out on the ice and in the stands. Envy and Greed get a workout when the players, their agents and even the club owners got together to talk about who's getting what deals, sponsorships, and whatever, and 'don't I' or 'we deserve the same or better?' I swear."

Satan took a big gulp. "Well, hell, boys," he said, ignoring Jesus' frown as he warmed to his topic, "even Sloth and Gluttony could get into the act with all the couch potatoes wedged in their easy-chairs, remotes clutched in their fists, stuffing pretzels and beer down their gullets as they flicked through layers of cable and satellite sports channels trying to watch all of the games. And, now and again, Lust would slink onto the scene during Stanley Cup season, and we all know what I mean, out in the street, when strangers meet, celebrating the sweet taste of their team's righteous victory and the other's deserving defeat."

The Devil paused again for another swallow of beer. He grabbed a couple of pretzels from a bowl on a passing tray. Munching and crunching away, the Ol' Boy looked somewhat thoughtful and sad. A few of the fellas found themselves thinking that maybe Mr. Scratch wasn't really so bad. Heck, give Ol' Nick his due, sure, maybe some of his reasons were wrong, but the love he shared with them for hockey seemed to be just as strong.

"It's not right," grunted Broda, as he drained off his glass. He handed off the empty to one of the angels for a full one like the way he used to pick up a long pass.

"No, it's not," agreed Satan, popping another pretzel in his mouth before chugging more beer.

"It is unfair," said Jesus in a still, small voice.

All ears turned to listen to the words of the Lord as he stood behind the bar, pouring out pints for the lads.

"It's not fair and it's not right," spake the Messiah. "But the Players Association and the club owners, they act in mysterious ways even I cannot understand, their strange wonders to perform. Even now to unravel the knotted snarl they have made of the NHL in time for the next season would be a true miracle indeed."

Silence followed this prophecy. Then a voice came from offside. "Do you think then maybe He...?" But the words died as Jesus shook his head.

"My Father, and yours, loves all His children, even those gone astray. But children cry out to be like grownups and have their own way. To be adult means to have free will. That means making choices and then there is always a price to pay."

Jesus began picking newly clean mugs from the washing machine tray, wiping out the excess water and putting them away. Silence descended once more on the room all around.

Then the Devil slammed his empty mug on the bar. The

glass exploded. Everyone jumped at the bang.

"I didn't come up here just to clear my own good name," he said, pausing to glare at a snigger from offside. "Fact is, some of my boys asked me to ask you guys if maybe you'd like to come on downstairs and cross sticks for a bit of pick-up hockey."

Everyone looked surprised. All except Jesus, who handed another tray of beer steins and pretzel bowls over to Michael to set 'round the tables.

"Play hockey in Hell?" growled "Lion" Labine. "With what? Asbestos pucks?"

Satan nodded. "I know, it sounds crazy, though I kinda figure even some of you Canucks might be willing to give it a shot under normal circumstances. But we all know that these are not normal circumstances." He paused. "Thing of it is, fellas, it's gotten a mite cool over at my place this season and, me, I'm kinda thinking this whole NHL freezeout may be part of the reason."

The Devil took another swallow of beer before he spoke again.

"The fact is, boys, Hell has done froze all over!"

Punch Imlach, a greater coach there never will be, glanced up from the table where he and "King" Clancy sat puzzling out chess. "So who've you got?" he asked. "Bunch of rub-dub rookies'd be my guess."

The Devil mentioned a few names. Triple A stuff at best, with a couple Flyers draftees who'd failed at the test.

One fellow hooted, another howled. Lucifer just stood there and scowled.

"I'm serious," he said, "and so's each one of my boys. They

may be mugs and thugs but it's hockey gives them joy. Sure, they're inclined to be rough, never took a bit of anyone's guff, but take it from someone who knows it's not every stickman can make the pros.

"So have a little pity if you would, for you know in your hearts that you should, and remember as you breathe that sweet Heavenly air that each one of you legends could have finished up down there."

Everyone had the grace to look shamefaced. Satan smiled with satisfaction though he put behind himself the temptation to gloat.

"What I'm proposing," said the Devil, "is a league all our own, one just for the fun, until it's time for Armageddon. Hockey the way it should be without any crap. No talk of luxury taxes or any salary cap."

He accepted another beer from the Lord and raised an eyebrow in question. Jesus smiled in reply as he lined up mugs for another drinking session.

"So whaddya say, boys?" Satan said, scanning the room all around. And on faces all over smiles broke through every frown.

So that's how it all came to be for the new D.H.L., with cheers ringing through Heaven for an idea born in Hell.

No one ever quite agreed what all the letters meant. "Hockey League" for H.L., was easy to tell. Maybe the "D" meant "dee-vine" or "damnifiknow" as far as anyone cared. The main thing was hockey the way it should be, for men with a yen to play shinny.

Lord Stanley himself, who gave us the Cup, dropped the

first puck to open up the new league in an arena on the outskirts of Hell. Smiling cherubs and tittering imps skipped after stray pucks and set the nets into place. Seraphim with swords of flame manned the goal judge seats while a crusty old demon drove the zamboni. The two Mary's kept score and the timekeeper's clock and kept things all sweet in the penalty box.

Jesus and Azrael were the linesmen. Not a bad combo at all when it came down to icing a bench-clearing brawl. If the Lord could calm troubled waters in a storm, then cooling down hotheads was no skin off his cheek. He spoke just a few quiet words and, like little lost lambs, they became all gentle and meek.

Azrael had no trouble with being heard though that melancholy soul never uttered a word. The roughest rowdy felt just a little bit colder at the soft tap of the Death Angel's hand on his shoulder.

Dropping the puck at centre ice was the One Who Loves Us All, and you know there's no argument when He makes a call.

There was even some space for Harold Ballard's sour old face. Satan smiled all the while as he presented the old man with a broom and battered dustpan. What a comedown for Ol' High and Mightyness to spend eternity cleaning up after everyone's mess.

That opening game was a white-knuckle match for sure with the time running out as Maurice Richard proved once again why he is the true saint of Québec. A new legend was writ large when Gabriel blew the charge, as Richard led a divine and rejuvenated Punch Line, dodging check after check.

Yes, the Rocket soared, that crowd of saints and sinners roared as Foster Hewitt yelled "He shoots! He scorrrrrressssss!" at a hat trick so slick, for with a quick flick of his wrist, Richard slipped the winning goal under Hell's own goalie stick.

Satan grimaced with chagrin but, with uplifted chin, stepped out of his team's box for a brisk little trot. On cloven hooves he skated to where Heaven's coach waited.

"Congrats there, Imlach," said the Devil, offering a hand to shake. "Maybe next time we'll win." Old Punch just grinned and said, "Why wait?"

Satan smiled back. Both coaches looked over to God, who gave His blessing with a nod. The roar of the crowd shook the rafters to the frozen ground as the teams settled down to play another round.

Now as far as I know, the games continue to go with every night a new show. The only problem they face is not lack of space but all of the players waiting in line for their own bit of ice time.

There's talk about expansion though, with plenty of players to go 'round, and there's future drafts to consider as well now with scouts flying out from Heaven and Hell.

More legends on Earth are getting long in the tooth. Won't be too long before Death draws up his own fantasy team list. It's pretty much of a cinch, when it comes to the clinch, that the likes of Cournoyer, Mikita, and Mahovlich will be sporting halos when they arrive. Ol' "Number One" Johnny Bower waits by the Gate to wave them in. Behind him stand "Big John" Beliveau and "Boom Boom" Geoffrion ready to hand them their jerseys.

And you can take it from me—'cause even the Devil would agree—that where hockey's concerned it's going to be Hull, alongside Howe, in a jersey for Heaven. It may be a long while before Gretzky gets the wrench but take it as gospel St. Peter's got the Great One's spot marked on the bench.

As for those "fine gentlemen" repping the NHL, both the players agents and the club owners, you can rest assured that there's plans for when they pay their dues. Old Ballard needs some broom hands to help with the sweeping around the arena.

Author's Note:

All of my brothers are confirmed hockey fans, and my dad (rest in peace) loved both the Habs and the Leafs. I am more of a canuck agnostic on the subject, as my own favourite sport is kickboxing but I understand how hockey works. Like most Canadians, I am still familiar with much of the past history of the NHL, and my story in this issue was inspired by musings about past hockey player strikes.

Mona Luna
Christina Ladd

If you never met her, you'd think she was a real nice lady, yeah. Good with kids, never kicked no dog. On Tuesdays and Thursdays she works down at the shelter, serving dinner, handing out socks and toothbrushes.

I go barefoot in my boots rather than take a single thing from Mona Luna.

Other folks call her Mona Blanchard, or Miz Mona. They say it with heads down, like they were praying. Some of them all serious, but some of them smiling.

Mona Luna always smiles back. She got this smile, yeah, it don't get you hot. It gets you *cool.* Cool like you got no place to be but you got someplace to go. Cool like an open hydrant in the Bronx summer.

One guy, he made a joke like her name was a dirty sound and everyone shut him up quick. Punched his arm, stomped his feet, hushed him so Mona Luna didn't hear.

I thought maybe I could talk to him, later. Tell him what I knew, see if he knew the same. But then I saw him take his dinner from Mona Luna. Just a baked potato in foil, he didn't want his greens. Wasn't hungry enough yet.

"Please take some," Mona Luna said in her low, sweet voice.

"You have to stay healthy."

She smiled at him. And I saw it. I saw him get caught. Hook in his mouth and it dragged his lips up until he was smiling too.

I never did talk to the guy after that. Wasn't any point.

Tuesdays and Thursdays I save my change for cans of pop, as much as I can buy. Tonight it's only one. I try to make it last.

"Hey," someone says to me. I recognize his face but don't know his name. Must be new. I know most folks round here. "Why you always coming if you don't eat?"

I shrug and drink my pop.

"Free country," says someone else. "Right Duffy?"

I nod. The pop will keep me awake, I hope.

"Oh, that's Duffy?" someone else says. "Shit, man."

I keep my eyes on Mona Luna.

She doesn't do it often. Not even every week. But you bet your ass she does it every month. Going on a year since she started coming, started taking, and I know she ain't never gonna stop unless someone stops her. And none of these poor bastards can see what I see. I gotta be as ready as I can.

Tonight she's handing out blankets and little bottles of shampoo that a hotel donates. I could take a little bottle, yeah. I could use a blanket. I know it's not the things she gives you, it's just her. But I don't want to. Men like me don't get too many choices. This one's mine.

The others, they go over, they get their stuff. They smile at Mona Luna, and she smiles back. But when they go back to sit, she frowns. Rubs her neck like it hurts. Blinks her eyes too much.

I see it all.

She rubs her neck three times. She stretches. Arms behind her back, and nobody catcalls, even though her titties press up against her shirt. It makes me shudder. Then she doesn't blink again, not for a while. She rubs her neck again, four times.

Not tonight, yeah.

•

Tuesday, though. Tuesday might be her night. I watch her close, and I got two cans of pop this time.

"Duffy, man, you coming?"

"Nah," I say. It's Greuber talking. Greuber was in the war too. People think we like each other because of the war. That's shit. War doesn't make you like people. War just makes you need 'em.

I need Greuber, but not tonight.

"C'mon," he wheedles. And I want to. He has good stuff sometimes. But Mona Luna, she rubs her neck, and I can't. I gotta make sure.

"Nah, keep it," I tell him. I gotta be sharp.

"Man, you going on that fucking wagon again? You?" He turns to the rest of the table. "This fucker, they dropped him on his head when he was a baby. Been falling off the wagon ever since, just to get the feeling back."

They laugh. I still don't take my eyes off Mona Luna.

"Ah, fuck you, Duffy," Greuber says, but he's not pissed. He knows he can keep my share for himself.

"Yeah, fuck you, Duffy," says someone else. "What you staring at?"

"New meds," I tell them, and they back off. Most of them

know how it goes. Meds will make you stare, make you laugh, make you cotton-ball numb. Nobody likes a man on meds.

Especially not me. I don't take 'em. Not anymore.

Mona Luna drops her shoulder. Rolls it. Then the other.

Tonight, yeah.

•

I wait for her across the street. She leaves with another woman, one with nice hair but a mean face. She's mean to everyone except Mona Luna.

"Oh, I forgot my bag!" Mona Luna says, smiling like her teeth never bit off a lie.

"I'll wait for you," said mean-face.

"No, no, you go on. You have Jenny's recital."

"It's not a good neighborhood…"

"It's fine. I'm parked right there."

Mean-face hesitates. But she does have that recital, and so she goes.

Now it'll happen, yeah.

Mona Luna goes back. She gets her bag. And when she comes out, she looks around. And there's Juke, right on the corner. He sells, sometimes. I know it. She sure knows it.

She goes to him.

My knees don't work so good anymore, so I follow slow, and I don't hear. But I see her pat his arm. I see her smile. I know he smiles back.

They go walking down the next street together. Juke, he's alright. He wouldn't take advantage. But *she* can't be sure, so what's she doing walking with him?

Mona Luna. The night makes her soft and shiny, a woman like we used to dream about. Back in the war.

I see them go round a corner, and when I get there I see just the swish of her skirt go round another. And when I get there, they're gone.

Shit. Yeah.

•

I don't see Juke the next day or the next, and then I can't be looking out because I have to see the doctor. I forgot last month and they don't let you get your benefits if you forget so much, so I take two trains. At least they got A/C.

The man down at the VA, he listens to my heart. Deep breath, one two. Let it out, three four. Have I been taking my meds?

Yeah, yeah.

He knows I'm lying. What can he do? There are ten guys waiting and only half have all their arms and legs. So he writes me some notes and talks big about shit he's never smelled, and he lets me go.

On the way out, there's Greuber again. "You seen Juke?" I ask.

"Who the fuck is that?" he asks back.

•

Juke's not *gone*, though. They're never gone. They just aren't there.

I see Juke and it's like the moon when it's empty going across the sky. He's in line for his food, and they give it to him and he takes it, and he's smiling that stupid smile. And he doesn't eat. And he doesn't sit at a table. He just keeps on smiling.

"Hey Juke," I say to him. "What's good?"

He looks over at me slow, and it's like he switched up his shadow and his body. His shadows, they all respond. His body is flat and quiet.

I don't want to, but I get closer. "What happened, Juke?"

The shadows around his eyes, those wrinkle cracks, they stutter. They move like the jungle used to move, straining in every direction. But he doesn't say nothing. Just smiles and smiles.

"Juke?" It's my last try.

"Who's he talking to?" someone asks.

"Duffy, man, you coming?" Greuber asks. And yeah, I'm coming. I fucked it up this month. And now I gotta wait all over again. Might as well fill the time.

•

It's more than a month, turns out. Mona Luna is always changing things up. But she never stops, so I can't stop watching her.

Juke is gone. Maybe he left, maybe he died: people can't remember and don't care. But I know he just went dark. So dark that now I can't see him either. But he's out there, all his shadows. Smiling.

And there's Mona Luna, smiling too. Now she's smiling at some kid I don't know. He looks like some of the kids I used to know, back in basic before they sent us off. Hell, he looks like some kid I used to be. And I think maybe I can will him to *see*, to not smile back. But he does.

I drink all my pop and crush the can in my fist. I got one more can today, and I got something from Greuber for the pain. I'm gonna be fast enough this time. This kid, he's on his way to being nobody, but he's not there yet. I'm not gonna let her take him all the way there.

Mona Luna makes her move early, though. She holds her belly like there's a baby or a pain, and the other workers nod at her. She leaves, but not before talking to that kid. And he goes with her out the door.

I thought I had more time. I was gonna find something, a brick or a rock or something, but I just gotta follow.

At least I got that stuff from Greuber. Cheap whiskey, toilet wine, who cares? It comes in a bottle, and there's not much left. I finish it as I follow. It helps me ignore the way my knees go off like firecrackers.

Mona Luna keeps going with the kid, further than I thought she would. Can she see me following? Can she hear me breathing hard? The streets are usually so long, but now it feels like the city is made of sharp corners.

But I'm good for it tonight, yeah. My knees can melt clean off for all I care. This is the jungle. This is war. No man or kid left behind.

I keep up with them until Mona Luna gets to a park. Then there's nowhere for me to hide, so I wait while they cross the street. But the light changes on me, and then I gotta wait too long for all the cars, and it's hard to get going again. I look down at my knees like I can get them to shape up. When I look back, I don't see Mona Luna.

Shit.

A second ago, they were by the big statue of some guy on a horse. Maybe they're behind it now, moving into the trees. I get as close as I can to a run, never mind the Fourth of July shooting up and down both my legs now, and never mind that I'm not hiding. They gotta be there. They gotta.

Around the base of the statue, I catch a soft curve of light like the twirl of a skirt. And I'm so grateful, I don't notice anything else for a second. But then I do.

Mona Luna is turning toward me. Smiling.

"Where's the kid?" I want it to sound like a threat, but it's just a wheeze.

"Oh, around." She tilts her head this way and that. "I'm more interested in you at the moment. You're the man who watches me, aren't you?"

"That's right."

"Duffy. That's what they call you, right?"

I don't respond, but she doesn't care.

"Yes. Duffy. But that's your last name. What's your full name, Mr. Duffy?"

I shake my head. I hold my bottle. But her *eyes.* They're dog's eyes. They just shine and shine with trust, and how can you look away from love like that, love you never had to deserve?

"James. Jim."

"*Jim.* It's so nice to meet you at last, Jim." I hate my name in her mouth. Like it's a sucker she's going to wear down to spit.

She moves, and I step back. But she's only holding out her hand to shake. I don't take it.

"Come on, Jim, I don't bite," she said, and she smiles. Smiles bright and gentle like the curve of the moon.

"How'd you do that?" I say instead.

"Do what?"

"Get my name."

"I asked you, of course!" She smiles like it's funny. She hasn't stopped smiling. "Even dogs greet each other."

"You *forced* me."

"Oh, Jim. I don't force. Do you really think I could?" Her smile is so bright and gentle.

"Yes ma'am, I do." I can't help the *ma'am*. When I'm scared my training comes out, and I'm scared, yeah.

She laughs. "Well, I *don't*. Never have. But—should I make an exception for you?" Her eyes are huge, too huge for a human face. I should hear her skull cracking to make room for those owl eyes. Moon eyes. Eyes like open mouths.

"No, ma'am," I tell her, calm as I can. You don't startle a wild animal. I know that much.

Her eyes don't go back to normal, but they don't get bigger. She cocks her head. The way she does it, it's like she jumped a noose. I almost hear the *crack*.

"What a funny man you are, Jim. Come, sit next to me. Tell me about yourself."

"No, ma'am," I say, but just barely. I'm so tired and my knees are made of napalm. I want to sit, but I just keep holding my bottle like it can hold me up.

"Well, all right. I'll sit, though. You don't mind, do you?" She doesn't wait for my say-so, though. She just sweeps her skirt under her and flounces down, pretty as a debutante.

I know I probably don't have too much left in me, and I gotta at least try one more time. "Where's the kid?" It comes out stronger, at least.

She looks up at me. She still has that puppy dog look, but dogs were all wolves and jackals, once. Yeah.

"'That kid' is mine. So are you, Jim. The mad and melancholy are all mine. I am *Umm Ghulah*, Empousa, queen of scavengers before Anubis ever took up the feather and the scales. I gather the dispossessed and the desolate, and I give them a place. With me."

I want to say, *like hell*. I want to say, *no, ma'am*. But I'm scared. I'm so scared that the bottle I meant to smash on her head, the bottle with no more relief left in it, it's too heavy of a sudden. I can't hold it. It shatters on the sidewalk, and all the pieces turn into brightness and shadow.

"Oops!" she cries. But she leans forward and stares into the scattered glass. "Look at that, Jim. That's your future. Don't you see it?"

It's hard to look away from her, but I dart my eyes down. I don't see anything more than broken pieces.

"Yes, broken pieces," she agrees. Did I speak? Or are my thoughts just at a pitch she can hear? "That's you, Jim. Pieces of you in the war. Pieces of you in the city. Pieces of you all over the place. And here you are—a shadow of your former self." She laughs at her own joke. It sounds like a whole pack of jackals howling at the moon. "In the light of day, shadows are just broken pieces scuttling around. Lost. But in the moonlight, shadows are part of the night. Don't you want to be part of something, Jim?"

I want to say yes. I want to say no. All I can say is, "part of what?"

"Part of me," she says, and she's brighter than anything I ever knew, but I don't have to look away. Such a gentle light. Such a pretty smile. She's smiling with her teeth now, and her teeth are sharp enough to bite my bones in two.

But I can't help it anymore. I smile back.

Citizen of the Galaxy
Evan Dicken

Editor's Note: This story first appeared in *Analog Science Fiction and Fact*, December 2014

The aliens were early. I swept the remains of my breakfast into the recycler and opened the door to find a gaggle of Uyuñi outside the apartment. They blinked at me, heads bobbing as my translator prism converted the binary flicker of their eyes into stilted Japanese.

"We have flown many kilometers since nightfall, is this Minato ward, Tanakawa district, one-five-three?"

I bowed to hide my grimace. Of all the species in the Sapient Milieu, the Uyuñi were my least favorite boarders. They were rude, and the oil from their feathers made the plycrete crack and flake. I'd have to flush the whole apartment after they left.

"We have purchased the use of your nest, Miss Mizoguchi."

"Sorry, we'll be out in just a minute."

The Uyuñi winked amongst themselves, their webbed feet making sucking noises on the concrete as they shifted back and forth. Their heads swiveled toward me. "We have decided to grant your request for time."

I shut the door before I said something I'd regret. Renting my apartment during the day to migratory aliens was the only way I could afford Tokyo on a teacher's salary.

I shouted for Mai. When she didn't answer, I went to her door and called again. Another few beats of silence and I slid the screen aside.

Mai knelt in the middle of her room, naked, the tiny LED's imbedded in her skin painting her body in sunset hues. Her hair was pulled back and plasticized, a line of faux gill slits picked out in mascara just below the shadow of her jaw. The only human thing about my daughter was the glare she gave me as I stalked into the room.

"Please put on some clothes."

Mai's fiber optics stippled her cheeks with flecks of yellow and green pique.

I darkened my prism before it could translate, and waited.

"Mom." The word was little more than a croak. How long had it been since she'd last spoken?

"There are Uyuñi outside. I don't have time to argue. You're going to be late, Mai."

"Nobody calls me that anymore." An alien name played across her forehead, the fractal interplay meaningless in any human tongue.

It was if there was a silken cord around my chest, tightening with every breath. She didn't even seem to care how hard I worked, how much I sacrificed. I crossed my arms. "You're not going to class without clothes."

Mai slipped on a loose robe, her expression flat as a frozen pond.

I watched her, wishing she'd shout at me, throw a fit, even break down in tears—something, *anything*.

There was a sharp rap on the window. An Uyuñi peered into the apartment, blinked, then gave the glass another impatient tap with its long, curved beak.

I waved the window opaque, flicked on the noise dampeners, and turned back to Mai. "I'm sick of this. Maybe if you spent more time with your own species—"

Her lips curled like she'd just bitten into a rotten fruit.

The door sensor chimed, and I squeezed my eyes shut. I could almost picture the Uyuñi outside, pecking at the console. "We'll talk about this later."

"There's nothing to talk about." She brushed past me and opened the door, fiber optics flashing a rainbow of apologies to the Uyuñi as she pushed by them.

"I just want what's best for you!" I wanted to go after her, but was pressed backward by the flood of squat aliens. By the time I made it back to the door, she was gone.

"Let me clear the apartment." I keyed in the commands and watched the plycrete swallow my possessions. The furniture and fixtures dissolved in a flicker of hard light, nanowire frames melting back into the projection plates.

When I turned the Uyuñi were all staring at me.

"Your nest is too small."

"The dimensions were in the listing, if you have a problem with the size—"

"You misunderstand. It is more than sufficient for our needs. We are referring to your hatchling. She should be given room to fly."

"I don't come to your nest and tell you how to raise

your...brood."

"Why would you? We are already very competent in that regard. You are the one in need of instruction."

I glared at them. "I want you gone before I get home from work."

That set off another flickering exchange among the aliens. I left before they could reach a consensus, thankful that the Milieu had yet to mandate doors that couldn't slam.

•

"So, why *didn't* MacArthur push to have Emperor Hirohito put on trial for war crimes?" I searched for whitecaps of interest among the sea of glazed eyes. Finding none, I followed an old teacher's cliché and picked the student who was paying the least attention.

Curtis Hong swiped a hand across his desk display, dismissing the chat prism that had been painting the air above its matte-black surface. There were a few furtive snickers from the rest of the class, but I pretended to ignore that he'd been kaleidologuing instead of digesting today's history download.

Curtis looked up, LED's flashing an inquisitive blue.

"In Japanese, please, Mr. Hong."

"Could you repeat the question?"

I did.

He fidgeted at his desk.

I let silence fill the classroom, hot and uncomfortable as a Tokyo summer. They didn't seem to care at all. Warmth crept up my neck as the argument with Mai resurfaced.

"What use are facts if you don't *understand* them?" I took a breath and started again. "To derive meaning from knowledge, from *anything*, we need to engage it. How Japan and America reacted to the post-war occupation can provide insight into the negotiation processes different cultures use to come to terms with—"

The bell rang.

My words were lost in the rustle of holoslates and feet scuffing on the tile floor.

"We'll finish on Monday."

They filed out in a jostling rainbow, silent but for the high, insect whine of spinning chat prisms and the occasional snort of laughter. I slumped back into my chair, vanishing the tridboard with a flick of my wrist.

A burst of color on my monitor announced someone at the door. Classes were over for the day and I didn't have any meetings scheduled. Maybe it was Mai. My stomach clenched in anticipation of another round of fighting.

"Come in."

Administrator Tan-Checkered Ochre Field whispered into the classroom on thousands of tiny tube feet. The Fostern stood a meter tall and was roughly twice as wide, the textured lump of its central body supported by five radial arms. It had no ears, nose, or recognizable face, but eyespots studded its dorsal surface, scattered like pebbles among the twists and curves of its hyperbolic geometry.

The chromatophores on Administrator Field's body shifted in whorls of casual greeting. I nodded back and retrieved my translator prism from the desk drawer. It was a bit old-fashioned, but like many who'd grown up pre-contact I'd never quite gotten the hang of Fostern. Even if it was the Milieu's *lingua franca,* the thought of having miles of fiber optic cable running through my body always made my skin crawl.

The prism hummed. "Educator Mizoguchi, have you time for dialogue?"

"Yes, of course."

"May I lay?" Field's tube feet caressed the edge of a nearby desk. At my nod it crawled onto the top, legs curling over the sides like a starfish prying open a stubborn clam. There was a hiss as the environmental rig Field wore surrounded the Fostern with a fine mist of vapor. A smell like wet autumn leaves filled the air.

"The Milieu Council on Education has decided the global history requirement is to be removed from the curricula of all member species."

I blinked. "Why?"

"We have determined that species history contributes to a parochial mindset. This runs counter to the Sapient Milieu's goal of fostering understanding among its members. These history requirements are to be replaced with new, broadly designed classes meant to educate future citizens about the Milieu as a whole."

"Wait, we can't study our own past?"

"Quite the contrary, human history will be included as a facet of Milieu studies." Field regarded me with a raised limb. "You are shading red."

"This is unbelievable, I—"

"As a member of the Council, I support the decision. The

Milieu is composed of forty two member species. Are you implying that human history and culture is somehow more important than theirs?"

"To humans, yes."

Bands of red and yellow indignation striated the Fostern's reply. "Your thinking is provincial. Human children will be better served by learning about those with whom they are to share the galaxy than by ignoring all but their tiny corner of it."

Field crawled down from the desk, pausing just before the door. "Course syllabi and relevant knowledge downloads have been delivered to your personal uplink. I suggest you take this as an opportunity to broaden your own horizons, Educator Mizoguchi."

My hands were cold against my forehead. If I resigned, they'd just find someone else. It wasn't like High School teachers were in short supply.

First Mai, now this.

•

Thankfully, the Uyuñi were gone when I got home. The apartment was a blank cave of grey plycrete studded with flickering projector plates. I pinged Mai while the rooms loaded my specifications, stepping onto the balcony to escape the smell of boiling plastic. My prism flashed green to show that the ping had been acknowledged, then went dark.

She was still giving me the silent treatment.

I slipped the crystal back into my pocket. The night was humid, but not uncomfortably so, the breeze carrying a hint of salt although the ocean was kilometers away. Gone was the heady mix of oil, exhaust, and hot asphalt I remembered from my youth banished by migratory flocks of free-floating scrubbers.

I shook my head. Had I just waxed nostalgic about air pollution?

The apartment finished its reconfiguration. Fresh fish and vegetables filled the stasis cube. With space at a premium, most apartments nowadays didn't even load kitchens, but I'd made a point of cooking dinner with Mai every Friday since she was old enough to handle chopsticks. Although it would've been easier just to order something from the food library, I wasn't quite ready to give up this one last domestic trapping, even if it was mostly symbolic.

I went through the motions of making dinner, Mai's absence like a missing tooth. Smells of hot oil, ginger, and *shōyu* conjured images of cooking with my own mother back in Kumamoto, the two of us hunched over the house's tiny gas range.

I'd only gone back home once since Mom died, stopping en-route to a conference in Nagasaki. The house had been replaced by a row of pachinko parlors, but I could still see the bones of the old neighborhood—the bump in Matsukoshi-dori, now paved, where I used to jump my bike, the faint smell of cherry trees along the banks of the canal, Mount Kinbō to the east, its ragged shadow pressing across the valley as if to scrape the whole city into the bay.

I wondered how Mai would remember our home. I couldn't imagine her coming back to the tenement towers and tearing up at the sight of the featureless box where she and I once lived.

Would she save the configuration in her personal files, maybe map it onto her current apartment when she felt sentimental?

I set two places. The click of chopsticks and the soft chuff of transport tubes outside only magnified the stillness. When my prism blushed a chatty red I embarrassed myself by how quickly I snatched it up. No word from Mai, only a message telling me that the new course syllabi had finished unpacking.

I poured myself a glass of wine and flicked through the downloads. Most of the classes concerned the Milieu's rise to galactic primacy, dripping with rose-colored descriptions of Fostern diplomats.

Pre-contact Earth history was summarized by the rise and fall of a series of increasingly large military Empires, punctuated by wars of ever wider scope and devastation.

It is as sad fact that humanity would have most likely destroyed itself long before achieving total, global equality and proper utilization of planetary resources. Fortunately, the Voyager I *probe breached their home system's magnetosphere on RG808.3, allowing for the Milieu to intercede and—*

I slapped the scrolling words away, my mouth sour. I paced around the apartment, started and stopped a few trideos, but couldn't seem to relax.

I pinged Mai again.

No response.

And again.

Nothing.

Agitation bled into anger. If she wanted to go, I'd make it easy for her. I blanked Mai's room, planning to box up her things and set them in the kitchen to scare some sense into her.

The plycrete melted back into the floor, holographic overlay flickering away to leave nothing behind. I checked Mai's closet and found it empty as well. Could she have come back during the day and taken everything? A quick scan of her usage records showed Mai hadn't logged any permanent possessions in months.

I reloaded her room, stepping in to inspect the facsimiles—a glass display of shells from a trip we'd taken to Enoshima, her grade seven volleyball trophy, a gallery of chipped and faded toys, the small tortoiseshell crane her grandfather had carved for her when she was a baby.

I picked up the crane and ran my fingers over the tiny notches my father had made to give the appearance of feathers— except he hadn't.

A soft chime stole through the apartment. At first, I thought it only wishful thinking, until my prism flashed green.

"Mom." Mai's face hung in the air, lips trembling, LED's dark. "I'm sorry for not calling sooner, but I didn't want you to try and stop me. I did it. I dropped out of Tōdai. I'm leaving."

I stumbled over to the prism. "What do you mean? What did you do?"

Mai's image talked over me. "I know you'll be disappointed, but it's my life, and my choice. Please try to understand."

It was a recording.

The memory of her empty room stung like a slap. I was still holding the carved crane as I bolted from the apartment. It slipped through my fingers in a fog of light, insubstantial as a dream.

•

Projected billboards crowded Obayashi station, plastering the air with advertisements for everything from "traditional" Earth cuisine to guided tours of our antique sewer systems. The central platform was crowded with aliens—although that wasn't technically the proper term for them as we were all citizens of the Milieu. The Space Elevator loomed overhead, gel-landers crawling up and down its twisted carbon nanotubes like beads of condensation on the sides of a long, thin glass.

I stood in the processing line, fingers picking at the hem of my blouse. The origin stamp on Mai's message placed it at the central platform less than an hour ago.

The line inched forward. I scanned the crowd for perhaps the hundredth time. Fostern, Uyuñi, and members of a dozen other alien species crawled, waddled, and floated amidst the managed chaos of the station. Human passengers—most of them young and naked—moved in small groups, their excited chatter like a sheen of oil on the fast-flowing crowd.

Tridvid projections above the terminal showed blurry protestors in New York and Beijing. Teachers with billboards shouted into the camera about the perils of whitewashing and cultural erosion. The scene shifted to a plain of dark red pumice dotted with structures like the shells of enormous conchs. A flood of crystalline aliens glittered along the buildings' tight spirals, the light from their bodies staining the sky with streaks of yellow and red. I didn't need my prism to know why they were angry.

My muscles hummed with helpless anxiety. Even if Mai were still here, I'd never be able to pick her out of the mass of almost identical youths. I should've gone after her as soon as she let my first ping slide, maybe I could've stopped her, maybe I could've—no, there was no way for me to have known what she was planning.

Unless I'd thought to ask.

"Would you do me the favor of presenting your Citizen Identification Colors, please?" Although he had a full fiber-optic suite, the clerk addressed me in polite Japanese. He looked to be in his early fifties, greying hair lined with plasticized highlights, laugh lines and crow's feet just beginning to bunch the skin around his eyes and mouth.

"I'm not here to travel. It's my daughter, she's going—" I chewed my lip. Where *was* she going? "I know she was here within the last hour, could you do a search by name and CIC?"

"Yes, of course."

I gave him the information.

The clerk glanced down at his console. "I'm sorry, I don't see any privacy waivers here. I can't tell you her destination."

"But it's right there."

He shifted the projection away as I leaned forward. "The Sapient Milieu respects the privacy of its citizens."

"But, she's my daughter."

"Miss Mizoguchi, your daughter is eighteen. The Milieu recognizes her as an adult. I'm sorry, I can't release the information without her permission. You'll be able to ping her via ansible once her ship reaches its destination."

My knuckles whitened on the edge of the partition, the collar of my blouse suddenly too tight. Even the closest worlds were weeks away by slipship. If Mai was going farther spinward it might be months before I could talk to her again.

The clerk's expression softened. "I *can* tell you she left on a Walkabout Visa, which allows free travel to any planet approved by the Milieu Council on Education."

His words blurred into a ringing buzz. Many of my students went on Walkabout. The Milieu advertised it as study abroad, but it wasn't. I'd seen the statistics—most of those who left never came back, at least not to stay. How could Earth compare to the galaxy?

The clerk gave a sympathetic smile. "Don't be worried. Your daughter went about it the right way. The Council only approves Tier One worlds, and the Visa provides for food and lodging. I see a lot of kids come through here without any plans to—"

I pushed away from the counter. Walkabout Visas weren't easy to get. Mai had the scores to qualify, but she would've also needed a recommendation from a Council Administrator.

I let the flow of the crowd carry me out onto the street, clutching my prism so tightly the edges left red divots in the flesh of my palm.

My fingers trembled as I keyed in the contact code, and waited, my tight-lipped scowl reflected in the prism's glittering facets. It was minutes before the acknowledgement came.

I leaned in close so the translator wouldn't miss a single word.

"Field, we need to talk."

•

I hadn't known there were any *McDonald's* left. Few old Earth chain restaurants had survived contact, put out of business by food libraries and matrix printers. Those that remained were small operations, catering mainly to aliens eager to sample the local ambiance.

Apart from the name, there was little familiar about the restaurant. It was situated on the edge of a pier, half-submerged in the calm waters of Tokyo bay. A mix of Fostern and other amphibious aliens stretched out on artificial boulders set at the waterline, catered to by humans in wetsuits stamped with the golden arches.

I waved away the hostess' offer of complimentary hip boots and waded in. The water's chill did little to dampen my anger as I sloshed over to Field.

"How dare you give my daughter a visa without consulting—"

My prism hummed.

"I'm over here, Educator, by the plastic clown."

I winced and backed away, stammering apologies to the confused Fostern I'd mistaken for Field.

The Administrator lay on a lichen-covered rock, several empty bowls of *nattō* spread on the table before it. I paused at the sight. The fermented soybeans acted as a mild intoxicant on Fostern. I hadn't taken Field for a drinker.

It gestured to a nearby rock. "Please, sit. Can I get you anything—saké, beer, wine?"

"No." Water soaked through the seat of my pants, sending an electric shiver up my spine. I didn't let it distract me.

"You had no right to approve Mai's visa without telling me."

"Where were you born, Mizoguchi?"

"Kumamoto," I blinked at the Administrator's question.

"This Kumamoto, was it once independent?"

"Long ago, yes."

Field scooped out another dollop of beans, twirling the sticky threads around its tentacle with practiced ease. "And when you were young, did you spend all your time studying Kumamoto?"

"Why are you asking me this?"

Field transferred the *nattō* to its beak and chewed for a moment. "There's been a great deal of resistance to the new history courses, even some riots."

"What did you expect? You're trying to erase our heritage."

"Not erase, *enhance*. Individual species are blinded by self-interest, unable to see the greater picture." Although the translator did a poor job with tone, I noticed the Administrator's colors were blurred—the Fostern equivalent of slurred speech. "You studied *Japanese* history when you were young because you were citizens of Japan, not Kumamoto."

"It's not the same."

"Isn't it?"

"No, it isn't. The United States occupied Japan for almost a decade in our twentieth century. They restructured our government and society, even rewrote our constitution, but that didn't make us Americans."

"Is that how you view the Milieu, as occupiers?"

I shifted on the rock, saying nothing.

Field waved one of the waiters over and ordered another bowl of *nattō*. "Are you sure I can't get you anything?"

I shook my head.

Silence stretched between us. The waiter came and left.

"I have three children," Field said, at last. "One is systems officer on an Explorator ship, another studies the interstellar migratory patterns of Uyuñi flocks. I came to Earth to be near the youngest—Single Red Dot is fascinated by your pre-contact waste disposal systems."

"Our sewers?"

"Indeed. I had hopes she would join the Diplomatic Corps." Field jetted air from its beak in a very good approximation of a sigh. "That's Mai's plan, you know. Walkabout is almost a prerequisite for anyone planning a career in politics."

"Politics?"

"I was honored when she asked me for a recommendation. She's a true citizen of the galaxy, your daughter."

My eyes stung. I wiped a knuckle across my cheek, thankful for the ocean's salty spray. I'd thought Mai wanted to be a teacher, like me. She'd always been so curious, so keen to learn.

"I'm sorry." Field's tube feet sketched abstract shapes in the condensation on the table. "It was selfish of Mai not to inform you, but she is young. I have no such excuse."

"You should've told me." I gave a sigh of my own, feeling the tightness in my chest uncoil. It wouldn't have changed anything if I'd known. If anything, I probably would've driven her farther away. "I'm glad you made sure she's taken care of."

"The Milieu cares for all its citi—"

"Don't push it."

"Galactic history is in the best interest of all." Field slumped down on the rock, arms drooping over the side.

I frowned out the window. Looking out into the night I wondered where Mai was headed, and if I'd ever see her again. "You can't force understanding, it has to grow on its own."

"But, riots? I don't understand—we've worked so hard, sacrificed so much to keep the Milieu together."

"You only want what's best for us."

"Yes!" the Fostern flashed, then went dark.

I laid a hand on Field's nearest arm. Its tube feet tickled my palm, then gently adhered to my fingers.

"What do we do now?" Field spoke in muted colors.

"Trust each other."

"But there are so many things your people don't know, aren't ready for. How can we be sure—?"

"Ask." I looked out across the bay, blinking back tears. There was nothing here for Mai, nothing but history. "You may be surprised what you find out."

The water glowed with light, a ghostly Tokyo mirrored in the rippling waves. And there, above the towers and tenements, in a sky clear as a sheet of tempered glass, was a diamond spray of stars.

"Field," I said without looking back.

"Yes?"

"I think I'll take that drink now."

Memories White
Matthew Donahue

I suppose he can sing, Miles. As much as anyone. Miles is the only other human up here. I never did get to hear him, but he told me he was quite popular out on the circuit.

When my head finally cleared, Miles said that the only thing that saved his life was that he recognized what they were attempting to do with him. Miles insisted that I should know what I was in for. He was always looking out for me.

"They took us into this little room—barely big enough for the three of us. It was me, that big purple jobbie out there—the one with the bunch of weird tentacle-type things that are always wigglin' around? It was me, him and there was this thin little pale fella with a big head and these big black eyes—"

"A *Grey?*" I said.

"Grey? Yeah, sure. I guess you could call him a little more grey than—"

"No, as in that's what they're called: Greys. It's the typical type of alien some nut would describe when they say they've seen a UFO."

"Hey, look at where you are, Chess, my man. Would you say there is anything nutty about aliens *now?*" He was sitting next to me while I was laying on the bunk in my pod—the pod I woke up in. "But, yeah, you got it. A little grey guy. Alien Classic! So, he was up first, but he didn't get it. Or maybe he just didn't wanna get it. So, they zapped him from the floor a little bit—not too much. Geez, he did *not* like that! His face crumpled up somethin' sour!" He chuckled at the thought. "Then, when it was his turn, the purple guy started blah-blahing along to the tune and quick— a real 'E for effort', I'd say. Then it came to me and let me tell ya, Chess, I belted it out the best I could! Gave them the works."

"Wait, where—is he still here?" It felt like I had only just gotten my bearings and I hadn't seen a Grey in any of the pods.

"Well, so they made us all try it again, but that classic alien fella, *he wasn't having any of it.* That guy didn't make a peep. Then, all of a sudden, the floor underneath him lit up major and they...they, like, you know, hit him with..." Miles was twisting his brow searching for his words. He made a "shocking" motion with both hands. "And that was it for him, man. No more of those types. I've seen a jack ton of different alien species come through here and if they don't make the audition—that's the last we see of them! Sometimes they like a kind and go and get another, but the second guy never works out.

"When it was Ol' Purple's go-round again, he sang it but with this clicking, hitching sound in his voice. I'm making an educational guess here, but that's probably what fear sounds like for him, for his kind. And now that's how he sings out on stage, and they love it. He goes on first every time. It really gets the bugs going. I haven't heard him sing different since before they killed the grey guy. Hell, I think it's safe to say that's probably true for all these guys with the way they sing. Scared t'death. So, when the song came back to me, I kept singing it as best as I could. Every. Single. Time. It's been good enough to not get me zapped out.

You'll see when you're in there—the big screen lights up their crazy words and you just follow along to the beat."

"What, like karaoke?"

"Yeah! Carry-O-Key! That's what it's called! Geez, Chess, it's been a minute. I would have never remembered something like that." It was clear that Miles hadn't talked to anyone in a long time, the way he jumped around in his stories and then rushed though parts. Sometimes he'd forget his words and there was a slight tremor to him, like he was constantly cold.

He continued: "You just follow along with the screen and it'll teach you the tune the way they want you to learn it, yeah? You'll know you're doing good when it stops and goes back to help you iron out some of the more...ahh...harder...?"

"Syllables?"

"Sure, Chess. Say, you're pretty good with words, you know that?"

I asked him if he was ever electrocuted by the aliens, but he shrugged it off. A high-pitched squeal sounded throughout the cabin and Miles bolted up off the edge of my pod. The constant hum of the ship took a backseat to a metal-on-metal sliding, grinding sound that you could follow behind the walls. The noise stopped at a tall, off-white floor-to-ceiling panel door on the main cabin wall. The panel lit up and flashed a single word in the aliens language. Miles, on the verge of a small panic, yanked me up on my feet.

"Okay, alright—the door says you're going in, Chess-man. Remember what I told you!"

"Wait, where does it say that? There?" I said, pointing to the twisted alien scrawl.

He tapped the chrome collar tucked under his chin, "It's your number, or name, or whatever."

"How the hell was I supposed to know what my number is?! There aren't any mirrors in this place?!"

"These sick bugs get off on being cruel, is what I think," he said, clutching my shoulders.

The door slid open.

"You'll do great, Chess. You go right in there and the light'll come on and you do what they tell you." He was squeezing my shoulders reassuringly like a boxing coach before the big fight. Despite his comforting tone, his skin was damp.

Inside, the dark room illuminated with a glaring thrum of clinical white light. Long and narrow with a low ceiling that grazed my head. The floor was divided into three sections. I imagined the crumpled up body of the Grey laying in the section farthest from me. The lights dimmed slightly except across the one longer wall. Then, the eerie, dreadful plunking of their music started and a hollow, less-than-angelic voice began to sing along with the strange looking language crawling across the screen.

I'm not a singer. I mean, I can hit lower notes alright, but my voice cracks when I do anything in an even remotely higher range. The utterly unpleasant sounding song ended only to begin again. This time I attempted to sing along with the cold voice. It had a pretty simple rhythm, like a "Frère Jacques" or a "Three Blind Mice", but a version written by, and sung for, maniacs. For quite some time I just stood there as I sang along, over and over, letting the tune and words take hold. The song would end and immediately start back up, every time. My legs were getting tired, after what felt like hours on my feet. I crossed my fingers and hoped that not standing at attention wouldn't get me shocked. The floor was cool and I continued to sing with my knees close to my chest. The voice had been getting quieter and quieter until I found myself singing the tune without it. It got to a point where I sang it all the way through three or four times without messing up completely before the song stopped playing and didn't restart. The room went pitch black and the door opened.

•

The last thing I remember was standing on a dock on a lake at night, looking at the stars. We were at Alison's parents' cottage and they were all asleep. I was away from the city lights, trying to catch the Perseids. And I remember seeing a streaking light that didn't move like a summer meteor. A bright white light took over the sky until it was no longer the sky, but a place. I was confused and my mind was scrambling to contemplate what was going on. My thoughts had been shattered white and rearranged. I'm still not sure of anything.

Was her name Alison? I sometimes say Anacin instead, but I think of yellow and dark green and know that's not her. I have these diffused images of her in my mind. They play on a loop that starts to stutter when I try to slow it down and concentrate. I try again, but can only recall an echo-form of what I was just thinking about. I try harder and that blinding, stinging white dissolves the memory almost completely and I have to take a break or my head starts to ache. I've attempted it so many times that now it all seems like just a memory of a memory; a story I've told myself of what happened before this place.

Now, the first thing I remember when I arrived was the deep lines on Miles' face. I was naked and cold and he was talking quickly.

"Hey! Hey, man! Do you speak English? Hablo Engleesho, pal?" He had a silver collar riding high above his Adam's apple. Something was etched on it that I couldn't make out. My teeth wouldn't stop chattering.

"Y-yeess-ss."

"Are you kidding me? That's great!" He gently smacked my cheek to get me to focus. My skin felt raw and his touch instantly brought me online. "Hey, man. You're okay. You're good, alright? My name's Miles, what's yours?"

"Ch-Ches-ttter."

"Chester? Nice to meet ya, Chester. Chester, you're probably gonna dip out on me soon, so you gotta listen to me, like, right now, okay? The aliens, the guys who took you? They want you to *sing*, got it? Just sing, like, for their people. On stage. That's what they got us doing here, so you gotta do it too, alright? It's not going to be good if you don't. You got it, Chess?"

It was difficult to focus on what he was saying. The bright white was still fresh and felt like static peppering the inside lining of my skull. A flea circus on fast-forward.

The room had a ceaseless, invasive hum you could feel penetrating your organs and bones, but never quite taking up residence there. I tried to sit up to look around, but Miles blocked my view with a calming hand to my chest.

"Nah, don't do that, man. Not right now. Just take it easy for the time being, alright? I don't wanna freak you *all* the way out. Not right away. Look, you're on board an alien space craft, *okay?* We were all abducted and so were you, and now here you are in a room full of all different types of aliens. You ain't seen nothing like it ever. *Trust me.* You're the only human here, except for me. It's just the two of us. Here..."

There was a bleach-white robe that matched the colour of the walls. It was like the one Miles and, as I would soon find out, all the other aliens wore. It was rolled up at the foot of the pod I was laying in, which, in my current state, part of me had confused with some fluorescent white tomb. He carefully dressed me. He knew my skin would be excruciatingly sensitive.

"It hurts, don't it?" he said. I gave a weary nod. "Just rest up a bit, okay? I'll sit right here with you."

As if these were the magic words, I fell back asleep almost instantly.

When I awoke, my flesh didn't feel quite as delicate. My head was somewhat clearer too. Miles sat cross-legged in his pod across the room, silently singing along to some alien script projected in his pod wall. I finally got a look around to see the others in the room, all tucked into their pods doing the same as Miles, but in different positions. An interstellar menagerie of impossible living things.

Each of the pods was a horizontal test tube set into walls. All of them were framed in a border that was lit-up when they were running through their song. I soon found out that when the light was off, you could hear the noises they made. Slick sounds and gurgles. Through the muted pods, it was harder to tell if some of them were singing at all since a few of them didn't have what you would call a conventional mouth.

•

After I survived my audition and the subsequent onslaught of rehearsals, I was returned to the barracks only to find Miles sitting on the edge of my pod. He looked relieved to see me again. The lines on his face crinkled in a fresh new formation. He looked like a dust bowl farmer who had just won the lottery. As the only humans in the room, we got to talking.

"While you were away, I was thinking. Now, I don't know how long I've been up here with them—I lost count at around fifty for all the different places I've played. And you can double that since then! You know, they even got a...paper...with my picture? For the show?"

"A poster?"

"Hell yeah! With my face on it and everything! You see, they like the way I *do it*—how I *sing*. I think I'm famous, Chester. I think I'm their favourite, wherever we go. I'm also thinking that they like me so much they might have dropped back to Earth to get another one, just like me. I mean, look at us, pal, we look *practically related* to each other, right?"

He wasn't wrong, we did look very similar. Same build, same hair colour, although Miles' had grown past his shoulders and he was starting to go bald. We were possibly the same age, despite Miles' weathered face and a shaggy, unkempt beard. He was a tarnished mirror image of myself.

"So do they like humans or just ones that look like us?"

"Well, they like me, that's for sure. Say, did you get the song that goes..." He trilled out the opening lines that I was familiar with to a sickening degree.

"I take it you've sung it before?" I said, wincing.

"Uh-huh. You know, that's what I figured. I think that one is their starter song or something. Everyone here knows it." Miles looked around at the others in their pods. All their border lights still on and all still preoccupied with whatever tune they were required to learn.

"Question for ya, Chess: what date was it when you were taken? You remember?"

"Ahh, that's hard for me, Miles. I've been trying to recall everything from before. It's all a little hazy for me right now."

"Right. I hate to tell you, Chester, but that ain't going away. I think these bugs did something to my brain, I can't remember a lot of things."

Miles went silent, the lines on his face folded in their natural, almost melancholy furrow. A conundrum of holding off trying to recall the past so that I still had some memories left, yet consciously ignoring those memories for fear of losing them.

"August...I'm pretty sure it was during the first week of August."

"Yeah? What year? 2017?"

"No. 2020."

Miles grit his teeth. "Almost three years. Gone. It sure as hell doesn't feel like it. You're the first person I've spoke to in...three friggin' years, Chess."

Suddenly the mechanical hum of the room spun down a few octaves and the gravity became faintly buoyant. Miles snapped his body up off the edge of my pod with the force of a hand touching boiled water. The other creatures began to stir in their pods. Some hurried, some moved heavy.

"We're landing. Okay, Chester, look: that panel over where you went through before? It's gonna light up with a list of what order everyone is going on." He hustled me out of my pod and looked me square in the eye. It was a look of desperation that I was starting to recognize in him. "Hey! *Do you know your song?!*"

"Yeah, I think so," and I rhymed-off the beginning.

An index of squiggles appeared on the blank door panel.

"Hey, is that the list?" I asked.

"Yeah, but keep practising. It looks like you're going on...third to last. I'm closing."

"You're the headliner then?"

He gave a helpless smirk, "I suppose so, pal. For a long time now. *Keep singing.*"

In the gentle gravity, I kept singing and Miles coached me along across some of the rougher terrain of the alien's more perplexing pronunciations.

In a nearby pod, a huge hunchbacked alien covered in a milk-coloured fuzz started to sing along with Miles and I under his breath. Another creature that looked like a cross between a fish and the long neck and wings of a scrawny buzzard—all scales and feathers—quietly, joylessly crooned along. When I slipped-up on a verse, the two started to bark and squawk the correct enunciation in an alarmed frenzy.

"Alright! Alright! He's *got it*! Chill out," Miles said, as if they understood English. "Like I said, everyone here knows your tune, Chess. They just want you to get it right, is all. I mean, we've all seen what happens when someone gets it wrong out there."

"Okay, I'll bite: what happens?"

The lines in Miles' face fell into their corrugated grooves. "There is no easy way to say this, but, the audience...well, they, like, *feed* you to them. The stage goes up and you slide right down into the bugs. They'll tear you apart—eat you alive. Those alien bug freaks love that song, so you can't screw it up, Chess, you just can't, *alright?*"

Again, he was clutching my shoulders.

"Yeah, Miles, don't worry. I'll sing it right," I said, because that's what he wanted to hear.

Miles smiled in relief. "Yeah, buddy. Let's do it again—you almost got it good."

Miles started from the beginning, slowing down and articulating the phonetically trickier parts. He really knew the song inside and out. While he was going through it, I wondered how many times he had to perform it live before graduating to a harder tune. What he must have felt that first time on stage—what all these creatures had felt their first time. And the fear they must associate with this song. I glanced around and wondered if all their faces truly looked this way back on their home worlds, or if they were changed forever by their experience out on the stage, like Miles.

And Miles. Three murky years of popularity and unable to fully connect with another sentient being in all that time. Just from my short stretch with him I'd catch a glimpse at what he might have used to look like before. It was when he smiled I could see it. With me in his life, he finally had somewhere in the world outside himself. Everything he knew about this place he could use and share with someone else. More importantly, he now had a friend.

The room minutely shuttered with a metallic *clunk*. The perpetual hum resumed its former intensity and the gravity settled back to normal.

"Alright, Chess. Time to get in line."

The others had already started forming a queue along the wall next to the door. Miles guided me to my place. I was standing behind some sickly turtle-looking thing with a partially transparent shell. I looked inside and through its cloudy liquid I could make out a miniature world of stars and galaxies. A whole cosmos in there. I wanted to ask Miles about it, but I doubt he knew any more than I did. The milky fuzz-covered mound of humps and muscles got behind me. Miles took up the rear.

"You'll do great, Chess. Just sing it like they taught ya and you'll do fine!"

The door opened and the line began to move. Miles began to sing my song out loud in a cheery "whistle-while-you-work" fashion. All of a sudden his energy was strangely upbeat. I sang along under my breath and the big guy behind me couldn't help but join in again.

We marched out into the dark beyond the door. Instead of the audition room from before, we were in a different place. Empty and dim. I could hear Miles from behind.

"This here's the back stage, Chess. No green room for us! Hell, we *live* in the green room, don't we?" He sounded remotely intoxicated.

The curved exterior of our ship was parked flush against the opening of the back of the venue. We lined up against a tall blank wall. I could hear the crackle of an audience on the other side.

Soon, there was an applause that sounded like someone balling up a bag of chips. Then an announcer that started with a pure hell-noise. I recognized the intonation of the language from my song.

The first in line—the nervous, shuddering purple tentacle creature—hurried his way out and around the far end of the wall and passed through a filmy curtain. I was feeling the anxious apprehension of just before you leap into a cold body of water. Jumping off a dock, holding Anaci—*Alisons'* hand and plunging down into the chilly lake on a hot day. No, that's not right—the top layer was warm. The cold was at your feet. In the lake. Alison? Yes, Alison. Applause from beyond the wall pulled me out of that moment of clarity. Was it gone now, the memory? I closed my mind off just in case and focused on the strange sounding music. I could hear the purple alien warble the begin phase of the first song of the night. I felt ill.

A dozen horrible songs later, it was the cosmic turtle's turn. He lumbered his way through the curtain. During the other performances I had been thinking, but not about my cruel tune.

"Hey Miles?" I called out, "what happens if I do alright out there?"

The milk-coloured creature continued to block my view of

him. "What the hell do ya mean? Well, for one thing, you don't die."

"Is that all?"

Miles thought about it. "No one wants to die, Chess. I know *I* don't."

The applause rose, then tapered off as the cosmic turtle began to sing, sounding much like how you would imagine a turtle would sound like if a turtle could sing.

"You think if you do alright, you'll ever get to go home?" I already knew the answer. It took Miles a moment to reply.

"No, man—I don't suppose that'll happen. I don't really remember what home was like anyways, so what's the point, you know?"

"And if you don't do good out there, you die. *That's it.*"

"Yeah. That's the long and short of it, pal."

"And if I do *really* good? What happens then?"

I thought he didn't hear me, or maybe he was ignoring my question. But I eventually heard him sigh and say: "New songs. Harder ones. They take up a lot of space, you know? Don't have room for much else. And we just keep going."

The song finished to atrocious applause. The noise was impossible to get used to. I heard Miles say: "Keep going..."

It was my turn. My debut. The announcer must have said as much because the audience went mad. Louder than they'd been all night.

"I'm sorry you're here, Miles. It must have been very lonely for you."

He didn't say anything for a while. "It's your turn, Chess," was all he managed to croak out. My name sounded different this time.

I peered around the milk-coloured creature over at Miles, but he was staring straight ahead. He had a tear running down one of the lines of his cheek. I couldn't think of anything more to say.

I walked out around the bend in the wall and onto the stage.

The auditorium was absolutely magnificent. Breathtaking, in fact. It felt bigger than any stadium I could have ever been in on Earth, although at the moment I couldn't remember any specific venues for comparison. It appeared to be a city-sized hall and it seemed that everyone in the galaxy was in attendance to watch this series of prisoners sing the songs of their people. From where I stood, my view of the audience seemed stretched and exaggerated, like the sensation of being under a massive microscope.

I finally got a look at our alien captors: insane gravel-skinned giants with trapezoidal jaws and large, deep-set eyes the colour of tin. Insect-like with humanoid features, as though a human being was struggling to morph out from within the body of a giant beetle and was painfully stuck halfway through the mutation; both the human and the beetle living a hateful, agonizing existence.

Seeing them now, the glossy gaze of their countless eyes, I suddenly could just tell that they were a race that genuinely enjoyed the sound of a voice wavering in fear. How they loved the singers' terror at the sight of the audience and how it affects the timbre of their performance. Or deeper still, the drawl of an exotic accent attempting to mimic the cadence of their language in sudden death. The natural clunk of a different speech pattern and the various attempts to synthesize our foreign sounds to their brutal music. I could see that they found pleasure in our struggle up here and tonight they were having a great one.

The song has just started now, but I don't. I try to burn off the rest of my memories of the cool water with Anacin until they finally slip out of reach. The bright white overtakes her image for the last time. I block the spotlight from my eyes. I focus on those jaws down there and I try to normalize the thought of having them tear into me. As big as they are, it shouldn't take long. I'm tricking my brain just long enough to forgo the terror waiting for me. They must really like this song, because when I replace the opening lines with a few blustering fragments of Earthman expletives, all those jaws just open and the sound is a dreadful, loathsome tone.

And they are howling now. All of them. And I can feel the stage beginning to tilt up behind me.

And now I'm sliding forwards, and any attitude I had about their giant jaws has disappeared. Now I see their size was always an optical illusion: the closer I get to the edge, the more the audience shrinks. I see that the size of the hall is far less than it first appeared and that these bugs down there are actually slightly smaller than myself. For them, they had my image minimized to fit their stage, but for me, on the other end, they seemed colossal.

And now I'm afraid this might take longer than I imagined. And I slip towards the very edge and I think of Miles and I wonder how long must the show go on?

The Alchemy of Curses
Joshua Grasso

1.

We started our morning round of visits. There were about twenty houses in the outlying village, many of them mere shacks that would topple in the slightest breeze (and a few that already had). Most of the families were as poor as we were—some even more so —but they still held their heads high when we passed, clicking their tongues with contempt. Near the center of town, however, were actual stone villas with balconies and gardens. Of course, we never stopped at their homes; they paid us in coins of the finest mint to avoid them.. Whenever we walked near their balconies they would follow us threateningly with their eyes, as if daring us to stop. Sometimes they called after us: *brikanji filth*! Once, when they weren't looking, I ran up to a door and spit on the handle.

Fever struck the house. Two people died that week.

Naturally, we were suspected and they chased us out of town for a few months. But where could we go? We survived on their alms, and as much as they despised us, they feared us more. They knew what we could do if we wanted. I didn't feel guilty for those deaths, since I didn't kill them. We never *kill* anyone. Our presence is like a sneeze; even if you cover your mouth, the spray flies everywhere, and someone is bound to get wet.

"Vikantanda!" my mother shouted. "Go see the Dubrovs. They haven't paid this week."

It was my favorite house to visit: a mother, her five nearly-grown children, and a father who was either dead—or drunk. They were scavengers, living at the very edge of society, but still of respected blood. Their ancestors had been warriors, men and women of distinction, and not the "bloodsuckers" or *brikanji* that we were. Of course, one could argue that their luck was equally bad, as they had tumbled several leagues from the sun while we hid comfortably in the darkness. The mother hated us, even threatened to shoot on sight if we came again (though we always did).

Since they were poor and troublesome my mother steered clear of their house, but I found any excuse to go—even when they pelted me with stones. Sometimes I got my trouble for nothing, but other times, I would catch a glimpse of the middle daughter, Jarmila. Once, she had to act as middleman since her mother refused to come out, her curses ringing through the creaky walls of their home. Jarmila apologized to my mother and gave us twenty crouck (a small fortune for them) and placed it directly in my palm. Even our fingers touched. I didn't wash my hand for days, trying to feel her impression and the intention behind it.

I later realized she offered such kindness to everyone, great and small. If I saw her from afar, she might smile, but the way you smiled at a child or a stray dog. I was one of many for her, all of whom she would scratch behind the ear or cradle in her arms. Still, I knew I could talk to her, if only we *could* talk, if I could ever get her alone. I just never imagined what I would say if we suddenly found ourselves together. Which is why my heart stopped when she signaled me from her yard as I passed.

2.

"Please, can I speak with you? I know you, though you might not remember me," she said, running up to her gate.

I didn't dare meet her halfway, since anyone—everyone— might be looking. *I might not remember her?* If not her, what else was there to remember in this wretched, half-spent world? At the moment I had even forgotten my name, but of course I knew hers. Though I was far too frightened to say it.

"Is it true...that you curse people? Not *you*, exactly, but your kind? The *brikanji?*"

I looked ather house, which seemed quiet, empty. She followed my eyes and smiled.

"They're all gone to church. I stayed behind. Don't worry, it's safe."

"If you really want to know...yes," I said, hesitantly. "Where we go, bad luck follows. For ourselves, mostly. But sometimes, we can give it to others."

"I wasn't sure. I just assumed people were jealous."

"Jealous?" I said, with a laugh. "Of us?"

"Yes, because of how you look. Your beauty."

Now I really laughed, despite my fear. Perhaps she was crueler than I thought; they all were, when it came down to it. Like a child pulling apart a favorite doll just to see what happened. That's how they looked at us, the ones who didn't curse us outright. Like a pile of broken toys.

"I'm not joking," she said, with a confused laugh. "Your

women are so beautiful, all dark hair and olive skin...we try to copy you, though they would never admit it. If you were less pretty, my people would forget who you are...they might even welcome your curses."

"You really think...but why? When you..."

I could only gesture at the obvious. Jarmila haunted my dreams, the pure jade of her eyes that emerged from the glorious tangle of red hair that spilled over her shoulders. She reminded me of the ruined statues you still found on the coast, with faces so real you wanted to kiss them—but feared they would bite back. I always wondered who placed them here, what god or devil thought such beauty belonged in this pigsty world where no one had eyes.

"You're very kind," she said, studying my face. "I've seen you passing my house so many times, but never thought to ask your name. Though I guess there isn't much time to talk."

"Ah, I don't think you could pronounce it. It's Vikantanda."

"Vikan...tanda? *Vikantanda*. That's not so hard. What does that mean in your tongue?"

"Something like *the far-seeing*. But there's not much to see here," I shrugged.

"I'm sure you see more than most. Which is why I need your help. How much would you charge...to curse someone?"

"Ah...that depends on who it is, and what you want done," I said, finding it difficult to discuss business with her.

"I want you to curse Ivan Glukov. I don't want him killed or anything, but a long illness—or an accident—that would be fine. However it works. I don't have much, but I saved here and there. I have thirty fobs—"

"Wait, please, are you saying...*Ivan Glukov?*" I repeated, still recoiling from the shock. "*The* Ivan Glukov?"

"I know, he's so important, the greatest landowner in the village and far beyond," she said, rolling her eyes. "Everyone worships him. Anyone would be honored to catch his eye."

"But not you?"

"I shouldn't tell you what I really think. If mama even knew I was here...my face would look quite different, I assure you. But no, not me. Not ever."

"Forgive me, but I can't...*we* can't. He pays us well, they all do. We don't even walk down his street. If I did anything, my family..."

"I can give you forty, I just need a few days. Even fifty, if that's what it takes."

Fifty fobs? Paying *two* would be a hardship for someone like her. I didn't know how to tell her that a thousand fobs would be insufficient for me to break our vow to the Glukovs. Many years ago, they paid us an enormous sum, I never learned how much, on the promise that "your filth never darkens my doorway, your smell never reaches my nose." I would do anything to help her, even put my life in danger, but such transactions were between us and the gods.

She read this in my face and her mouth stiffened. I could see the pain in her eyes, the feeling of helplessness when not even money could save your life. Before I could respond we heard voices—her brothers coming up the hill. She wanted to stop me, to say something else, but I gave a hasty bow and departed. I had already put half a mile between us when I heard them questioning her, demanding to know what I wanted. So that would be the last time we spoke. I would never return to her house; she would quickly forget my name. The next time we met she might have good reason to hurl a stone with her sisters.

3.

Several days passed, but that brief visit haunted me to distraction. I couldn't read, I could barely eat, and I only slept to dream of our conversation. I briefly considered visiting her house again, but even adoration had its limits. My people would never allow it. If they saw me chatting up one of the Fiolkas I could be exiled from the clan. As much as they hated us, we despised them; my own mother said they were unclean and deserved whatever curses we gave them. While I could never hate them, there were times I could see her point. Deep down Jarmila was just the same, and she would become hardened and bitter as she grew old. Eventually, she would teach her children to hate us.

"Look," one of my brothers said, smacking my arm. "It's that Fiolka girl, the one who smiles and says good-day like she gives a damn."

I gasped. She was walking towards us as we rested under the shade of an oak. My brother watched her approach, then cut me a sidelong glance.

"You...know her?"

"Not exactly. We talked—only once. Please, let me...don't say anything."

He threw up his hands, as if to say, "by all means, get in bed with the devil. Death comes for us all."

I quickly got up and walked towards her, almost waving, but fearing she had come for revenge. After all, I had refused her request...and she *was* one of them. My fears left when our eyes met and she smiled in recognition, as if we shared something deeper than mere acquaintance. As we met, she made an awkward gesture and said something about the weather, which I was too flushed to answer. Seeing my discomposure, she gave a slight laugh and asked if we could talk.

"Isn't it dangerous for you to be here? To be seen with me?"

"I'll take my chances. What about you?"

Seeing that I had no objection, she continued right where we left off: "I already know your answer, and I know it's unfair of me to ask again. But you have to understand why I'm asking. If you understood, if I told you everything, I'm sure you would help. Money is no object. I'll find whatever you ask."

She stared me down, so I nodded my consent to listen—not to help, but to listen. I sensed a quiver of hope in her voice. She began her tale.

"My youngest sister, I'm sure you've seen her. Her name is Zdenka. She's about to turn fourteen."

I nodded, remembering how the youngest daughter once threw a rock that knocked off my cap. A very cute girl. She smiled with crooked teeth.

"Ivan Glukov paid my mother to see her...alone, you understand. The way he paid for all of us; me, and my sister, Olga. I was barely thirteen when he paid for me. But now...I want to be the mother I didn't have. I have to protect her—I can't let him take Zdenka, too. She's so young, she still trusts people...she still trusts me."

Her voice cracked in a sob and she covered her mouth. I didn't know what to say, but it didn't surprise me. He was a notorious skirt-chaser in the village (or so I heard). I only wish he had spared Jarmila. And more than ever, I wished I could curse him within an inch of his life. I wished I could kill him.

"If he could get sick, or injured in some way, maybe he would forget her. At least long enough to get her out of the village. You see...she's like my own daughter. I've practically raised her myself. My mother...well, you know what she's like. She'll sell any of us for a profit. That's where I got the money. It's what he paid her. I stole it...she hasn't noticed. But I'll give you everything he gives us—more even—if you agree to help me. Please, Vikantanda."

I spent days thinking up various responses to her pleas for help. Some of them 'yes,' others 'no,' but all of them ended in tears, and a few—melodramatically—with kisses. But I forgot all of them now. I had nothing I could possibly say to her. Only the truth.

"I would do anything to help you, Jarmila. But it's not just me. I'm part of my clan. What I do affects us all. They would never allow it."

"You know my name?" she said, genuinely surprised.

"Of course. Why wouldn't I?"

"Because...I just didn't think you noticed. We're so awful to you...why would you care?"

"I generally don't. But I've always noticed you."

"I'm quite touched," she said, studying me sadly. "And you're sure? There's nothing?"

"If I went near his house, and he got sick, the entire village would be up in arms. We might curse them tomorrow, but they would kill us today. There's no other way. *Unless...*"

"Unless?"

I had been thinking out loud, letting my thoughts lead me into dangerous speculations I had no business thinking. Sheepishly, I admitted there *could* be a way to curse him, a way that would absolve me from all responsibility; but it would demand much more—too much—of her. I tried to mutter apologetically, but she insisted, gently tugging my arm. *Go on, tell me...*

"Our curse spreads the longer we stay in one place, which is why we keep moving," I explained. "But there are rumors that some people who traveled with the camp—that is, non-*brikanji* who became lovers, wives—gained the power themselves. At least some of it, for a short period of time."

"Wonderful! How do we do it?"

"To give it to you, I would...ah, have to touch you. For several minutes, even an hour, perhaps. I'm not sure."

"Touch me?" she said, with a grin. "Ah, I understand your hesitation. You think that I might refuse to touch you...as a *brikanji?*"

I nodded.

"I don't mind at all. I would do anything to save Zdenka. When do we start?"

"Not here, not *now*," I said, looking back at my brother, who continued to watch. "Can we meet somewhere tomorrow?

Somewhere difficult to find?"

"I know just the place. By the ruins of the old castle. There's a cave, do you know it? No one ever goes there. First thing, at dawn."

"Perfect," I agreed.

She seized my hand and squeezed it by way of thanks. Then she scampered back up the hill to her village. As I watched her go, my brother came up behind me and said, "their women are like vampires once they smell blood. And she looks hungry."

4.

My brother was as good as his word; he didn't tell my mother or anyone else in the clan, though he gave me dark, 'I warned you' looks all evening. I counted the minutes and of course didn't sleep a wink until dawn. An hour early I stole out of camp and raced through the shadows toward the silhouette of the castle on the horizon. The castle itself was avoided by the villagers as an unholy place; ghosts were said to haunt the grounds, as much blood had been spilt in the godless past. Without difficulty you could find pieces of bone, an almost intact skull, many of them still encased in armor as if the war was in intermission. I much preferred our own age, where hatred lived behind closed doors and rarely emerged to settle scores, even if the sum was passed on to future generations.

I found the cave without difficulty and long before she arrived. It gave me time to consider what I was doing. I could fool the village, perhaps, and even myself, but what of the gods? Would they smile indulgently on my transgression? Or call it for what it was: a cheap excuse to hold her hand?

"Vikantanda!" she whispered, ducking into the cave.

"Here," I said, guiding her to my voice.

She sat down beside me, catching her breath. She brought a whiff of eglantine which reminded me of her house, the many days I would wait in the bushes, hoping for a glimpse that never came.

"I had to run...my sister wouldn't sleep, and kept asking me questions. I finally had to make up an excuse. I hope I'm not late."

"Not at all...it won't be light for some time yet."

"Then should we get started? What do I need to do?"

"Let me take your hand. That might be enough," I suggested.

She agreeably offered it up. I touched her fingers and immediately lost sight of the plan. As my eyes accustomed to the darkness, I could make out the contours of her hand, the small, yet strong arm that led to her sleeve, the eyes that watched it unfold. I pressed her hand and she returned the pressure, anxiously. Time passed as we sat in silence, waiting for the alchemy of curses to take effect.

"Do you think it's working?" she asked.

"I'm not sure...do you feel wretched? Like one of the damned?" I asked, with a grin.

"Is that how you feel?"

"Most days. But I don't think that has anything to do with the curse."

"Nonsense...you're not damned or forsaken or anything so foolish. You're not even *brikanji* to me."

"Really? Would you let your sister marry one of us?"

"If she loved you, of course. Though she would probably have to leave the village. My mother, for one, would strangle you both—and me, for being the matchmaker."

"No, not me—but someone else. Another *brikanji*. It's easy to say, *oh, he's different than the rest, not like the others*. What if she fell in love with my brother or one of my cousins? Someone with even darker skin?"

"You have brothers? Sisters?" she asked.

"Yes, one of each. Could you imagine that—having *brikanji* for sisters-in-law? Would you wear the traditional wedding dress? Sing the traditional songs?"

"I don't know your songs. Could you sing one?" she asked, amused.

"It's not something you sing alone. It's more like a chorus."

"Then teach me. We can sing it together, while we wait."

"It's a *wedding* song. And actually, it's a little...er, risqué. There's a part about the wedding bed...and the size of...the bridegroom."

"Even better," she laughed.

So I taught her the song verse by verse, taking care not to translate its meaning, and blushing furiously as she sang—quite beautifully—the line about the bridegroom 'rising' to meet his bride in the bedroom. We sang it several times, over and over, until we dissolved in laughter.

"Are you sure it's working like this?" she asked. "Shouldn't I feel something? Is that how it works?"

"It's true, this isn't much contact. Maybe if...I embraced you?

You would get a lot of the curse like that."

"Good…I want him to suffer."

She slid closer to me and threaded her arms around my body. The smell of eglantine and other scents—the musk of sweat, the richness of hair—was overpowering. I held her in my arms and felt like I was floating through the cave and into the castle itself, as the sky brightened with a thousand colors.

"I meant what I said…I would let any of my sisters marry you. I'm not like the others."

"Wonderful—one less stone to duck."

"This power you have…are you sure it's a curse? I know it can cause bad luck, but can't it help people as well? Aren't you helping me?"

"Anything can be bad or good, I suppose," I said, as her hair tickled my nose. "But it's never brought us anything but pain. I would be well rid of it if I could."

"But it brings you money—it gives you a livelihood," she said, excitedly. "I wish I could do something other than tend the cattle and take my mother's abuse. I would use it to help people, my sisters, anyone I could."

"It's not that easy…bad luck spreads, you can't control it. It's like what happened at the castle: you fight a war to save the land, and both sides perish. Maybe one side loses a few less people…but you're all covered in blood."

"Then we're all cursed, we all suffer," she nodded. "And we all throw stones."

I could feel her tears against my neck. I held her tighter, wanting to find some way to contain it, to trade my curse for her pain.

"I'm sorry...for what happened to you," I said. "You didn't deserve it."

"I was young—it's easy to forget. But I won't let him do it again. I just knew...even before we spoke, that you would help me. You looked so kind, so perfect. So beautiful."

"Beautiful? Don't you mean our women?"

"You had a mother, didn't you? But I noticed you the first time you entered the village. I couldn't stop staring at you."

"I never noticed...I never saw you looking. And I looked a lot."

"Not enough. Because you would have seen me," she said, nose touching nose. "My sisters teased me—*looking for that brikanji boy again, are you?* That's why Zdenka threw rocks at you. She was jealous."

"Funny," I said, as our lips met. "I was always jealous of her."

"Of her? Why?"

"Because I knew you loved her."

When she finally pulled away, birdsong intertwined with the violet rays of morning. We both knew she had to go back, and I would soon be missed as well. Our arms moved apart but our hands wouldn't let go. I pushed her away; she pulled me closer; I did the same. She finally kissed me on the head and let go.

"I think it worked," she whispered.

I watched her slip out of the cave and into the trees that lined the castle.

5.

I didn't hear anything of Jarmila for the better part of a week. I lingered by her house but only saw her older sister, Olga, who studiously ignored me. I glumly went through my round of the houses, often not even waiting for alms. A villager finally called after me, as I was slinking off,

"Don't you want this?"

She anxiously offered me a few fobs, extending her arm as far as it could humanly reach. Out of kindness or boredom I took one and declined the rest.

"And you won't...?"

"No, Great Mother, I won't darken your doorstep with curses."

"Oh, thank you...it's just when I heard about the plague I got so worried. I didn't want you to think that I was being uncharitable to such...*good neighbors*," she said, swallowing hard.

"Plague? What plague?"

"Haven't you heard? One of the great nobles caught it. No one else in his street—*yet*. He's in bed full of boils and raving and sending for doctors as far as Belladonna. They said he might die come morning."

By the gods—she had done it! But I trembled at the thought of what she had accomplished; even haunting his property for days on end might cause him to break a leg or have terrible dreams, but the plague? That would take far greater intervention. Her powers must be considerable to strike him down after a single meeting. So why hadn't I seen her? Surely he would never suspect her, and even if he grew suspicious, the symptoms wouldn't appear immediately; she had plenty of time to return home.

"And it's affected no one else? Just the gentleman?" I asked her.

"As I said, no one else in his street. Just him and his servant; she caught it first."

"His servant?" I said, with a start. "What servant—a girl?"

"I think so, yes, some girl of the village. Probably she picked it up by consorting with some filthy *brikanji*—oh, not you, good neighbor, I would never suggest that!" she said, with a guilty smile. "Ah, I meant one of the more disreputable types."

I nearly fainted in her arms. The woman gave a snort of derision as she helped me up, but offered to fetch me water. Once I recovered myself I stumbled toward the forbidden streets of town, hoping to trace my way to the Glukov estate. Dusty roads gave way to signposts and cobbled streets. People stared at me with open-mouthed contempt, but I was too dazed to respond. A coach nearly ran me down, the driver striking me with a horsewhip as it passed. I tumbled into the gates of a respected household, prompting a servant to lay hold of me and hurl me into the street. I resisted, wrestling him to his knees. As we struggled, a small crowd watched in mute excitement.

"*Brikanji* devil! Come to extort our master?"

"I want nothing to do with your master! I'm looking for the Glukov estate."

"Are you, indeed? Look here, citizens! This scoundrel wants to pay a visit to the Glukovs!" he cried.

"Yes, to finish the job," someone shouted.

"Let's escort him! Make him eat the curse he gave to Glukov!"

Three men grappled me to the ground and subdued me. I only offered token resistance; if they could take me there, if I could see her once more, what mattered if I lived or died? Especially when she might be dead already. They marched me a few houses down, a crowd gathering in a frantic, holiday spirit. A few people spit at me, others ripped at my shirt, though none of them knew my crime—other than being a *brikanji*, of course. In that case, guilty as charged.

They thrust me into a vestibule where several men were consulting with a doctor, all of them wearing gloves and masks outfitted with vials of nutmeg. The doctor no sooner caught sight of us than he began shoving the nearest intruder.

"Are you crazy? Do you want a mass infection? This entire house is under quarantine!" he protested.

"But this filth—he's the one who cursed them! The *brikanji!*" the servant insisted.

The men shrank back in horror, though the doctor only retreated half a step. Peering at me from beneath his mask, he asked me a series of questions which made no sense—possibly in Latin. He shook his head impatiently, then seized my arm and examined my pulse. Everyone waited with bated breath, though for what, I couldn't imagine. He suddenly dropped my arm and removed an instrument which resembled an astrolabe; he used it to trace the outline of my body and measure my forehead. After adjusting a dial on the center, he repeated these actions. As far as I could tell, nothing changed.

"Leave him. I'll take him to the master," he said.

I allowed him to drag me along, hoping to see if there was

anything left of Jarmila. Perhaps she could still walk; then we could flee this place and hide in the mountains. They would never pursue us, not in her condition. I didn't fear catching the disease, and besides, we had old remedies for the plague. And even if we died, so long as we died together...

Ivan Glukov sat in an armchair, his arms and legs covered in medicinal wraps, his face a series of blisters. However, he hardly seemed to be at death's door, and was calmly sipping tea before the fire. The doctor coughed to alert our presence, and the gentleman looked up with confused embarrassment.

"This *brikanji* claims he brought the plague," the doctor said, with a dismissive gesture. "Though as I can see no signs of the illness, I have serious reason to doubt—"

"So you're *Vikan-tanda?*" he said, with a tilt of his head.

I had trouble swallowing my surprise, so the doctor obliged by saying, "*you know him?*"

"You can leave us. I was hoping to speak with him."

The doctor made what I assumed was a look of exasperation before departing. Ivan waited until he was out of the room and gestured to a nearby ottoman.

"Please, sit. I insist."

"Where is she?"

"Dead. Or close to it," he said, lowering his head. "Whatever she did to me utterly consumed her. She's been in and out of consciousness all morning."

"It should have been you. She told me...I know what you've done," I said, staring him down.

"Whatever she told you, it wasn't the truth," he said,

lowering his cup to the saucer. "Not that it absolves me. Because you're right. It should have been me. If we could trade places…."

I sat—or more accurately, collapsed—on the ottoman. Something about how he said it…I almost believed him.

"I suppose she didn't tell you…we were in love?" he said, with considerable effort. "It was a grand romance. I even toyed with the belief that we could run off together, be married. I was foolish enough to tell her, too."

"Impossible…you did terrible things to her, and her sisters. From childhood," I said.

"I never touched them. Only her…when she was old enough to make her own decisions. I fell for her instantly. Her beauty, of course, but something else…she seemed to know things before I said them. So wise, that girl. Pity she was born here, among our lot."

"I don't understand. She came here to kill you—for revenge. I helped her do it. Why would she kill you if…you were in love?"

"Because she was willing to sacrifice everything—and I wasn't," he said, taking another sip. "She begged me to take her away from this place. She hated her sisters and the village. Hated her mother even more. I promised I would, but you know, I never intended…I don't know what I intended. I just wanted to enjoy her—to enjoy us, for the moment. I thought she understood."

I suddenly remembered her words in the cave: "Good…I want him to suffer." Nothing surprising, but looking back, she said it without the venom I expected; more like a woman who had lost everything and wanted it back.

"My aunt caught wind of our dalliance—demanded I drop

her immediately and make a proper alliance. Even found me a woman, too—the *bitch*. So I tried to break off with her, but the words got twisted up; I said she could still be with me, but just not my wife. I could find her a place in town, and would visit—occasionally. Jarmila threatened to kill anyone who took my name, wife or offspring. So I gave her money, enough to leave the village on her own. But the way she looked at me, I knew she would be back for blood."

I didn't say a word. There was nothing to say. I merely stared at my boots and waited for the world to end.

"I can see you were in love with her, too," Ivan said, struggling to change his position. "I'm sure, in her way, she believed what she told you. I could never tell exactly what she was thinking. Maybe she never loved me at all. I'm only sorry she didn't succeed."

"Can I see her?" I asked, standing up.

"She's in there...but there's not much left," he said, with a weak gesture.

I had almost reached the room before Ivan called me back.

"I think it's time your people moved on. I won't make an issue of this, but word travels fast. There's bound to be repercussions."

I nodded and felt my way into the nearly pitch-black room; only a few candles flickered weakly on an alcove. On the bed, I could see what remained of Jarmila wrapped up, scarcely breathing, stone white in the gloom. I anxiously approached the bed, wiping away clumps of hair draped across her face and arms. She turned to one side without being aware of my presence. The disease had extinguished her life; even I couldn't help her now. I felt utter despair instead of rage or indignation. I said her name a few times. Dimly, she peered through the veil of sleep; a half-smile, a weary expression.

"Is he dead?" she asked, in a rasping voice.

"No, he survived."

Her eyes closed in pain. When they opened again, she seemed resigned to her fate, distant.

"You're still beautiful," she said, looking up at me. "You always were."

"You lied to me. Why?"

"Because...I wasn't allowed. Like everything else. I only had one life...not enough for this place."

"I'm sorry the curse didn't work."

"It worked. Just what I paid for," she whispered.

And that was all. Whether she died then or lived a few more hours, I couldn't tell. She slipped out of consciousness as I left the room and I never looked back. Nor did I share another word with Ivan, who tried to stop me with a mumbled apology. I walked past the doctor and his assistants, who warned me not to return; the villagers were already in council—they didn't take plague-bringers lightly.

"One day, your luck's going to run out," a servant said, as I passed.

I turned around and spit on his shoe. He leapt backwards and stumbled, wide-eyed, into the doctor. I spit once more for good measure. I didn't want to leave any trace, assuming the curse still worked, assuming I was still *brikanji*. Though I could never be as good as her.

I heard the news from a coachman a week later, drunk, exiled from my clan. The entire neighborhood had burned down overnight. The *brikanji* would never return.

He Sold What He Had Left
Diane Callahan

Just a pinprick, a little
poke in the eye, barely feel it,
Prisoner 373, you'll barely feel it.

The needle slides in real familiar
thin as a hummingbird's tongue
through the brown of his iris

and the needle's nectar drops
steel doors over his mind.
In that dark room he remembers

the cold concrete steps, mama's voice
upstairs faraway, a green balloon
flies high as the penthouses where
maybe they see him as a colored
speck below.

Then the choking heat of the greenhouse,
picking raspberries all year long,
palms stained pink like a slap.
The bossman sniffs the air, says
some dirty rat has been getting fat
on the inventory, and eyes rove

over, fall on one person, but the next

motions blur into a watercolor of sensation:
shouts sharper than a bite, that green balloon,
mama's raspberry pie, soft throat
yields to hard fingers, a lingering
metallic cloud fighting against the sickly
sweet berries

and these jagged pieces of himself
will be sold to the highest
bidder because memories equal
commodity, a thrill ride for deeper
pockets who live in cities constructed
from pixels not steel, or for the probing
questions of white-walled scientists
studying the why, how, not again
of his stained hands.

He gives not as a confessional,
not as a bid for freedom but
because he knows it's worth something—
and it's better to be worth something
than nothing at all, so

he signed his name, swirled
his fingertip across the glow
to earn his twenty bucks.

Just a pinprick, a little
stab in the heart,
you'll barely feel it.

Grass Whisperer
Lynne M MacLean

The grass whisperer appears at daybreak.
He crouches in the shadows,
Watched by a lone and silent hare beneath
The dawn-shivered pine;
A huntress cat pads her way home,
As the first birds catch their breath between twittering exhalations.

Only his hands move,
Long fingers digging,
Face close to the earth,
Coaxing shoots, rooting out weeds,
One by one by one.
More birds raise their voices, crescendo,
And the grey sky flushes rose.

Dressed in loose drawstring pants,
And an old t-shirt,
Wafting scents of tobacco and tool shed and sleep.
Tall, reedy like the faraway grasses of his youth,
High grass that browned in the hot summer days
And endured the long winters through.

He's been transplanted now to a rainier clime,
One more place to sink relentless roots
Penetrating time and distance and half-revealed echoes
Of insistent generation.
His ancestors tended oaks and mistletoe and holly
In deep dark forests that whisper answers in his dreams.
He vanishes as the sun climbs,
Fades into everyday skin and
Clothes and public smiles,
Into neighbourly toil and banter.

I rise before dawn,
Or our paths will not cross again until sunset.
Sunset, when he emerges briefly to shush the grass,
When I sit in the garden, in the gloaming,
In the long, dense shadows,
Murmuring to the night bloom,
Beckoning the moths,
Calling out the fireflies,
Watching, as he passes into the night.

Author's Note:
This poem was inspired by gardening, which is really quite a
mystical activity. Why do you think roses require all that blood?

After Dinner Conversation is a growing series of short stories, and audio and video podcast discussions, across genres, to draw out deeper discussions with friends and family. Each story is an accessible example of an abstract ethical or philosophical idea and is accompanied by suggested discussion questions.

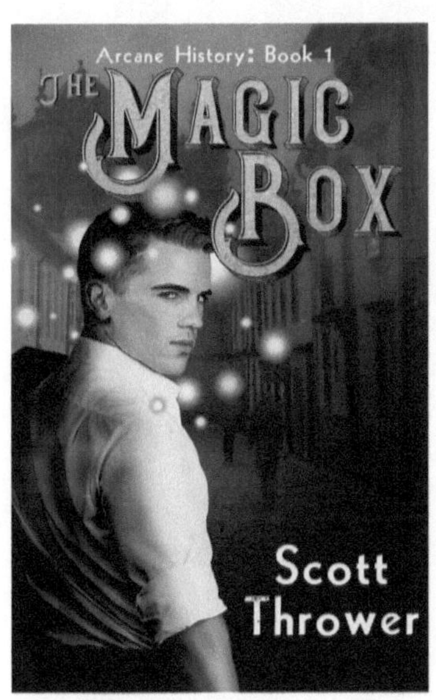

The one thing that could save his life might also end the world.

When Charlie's called away from his history books to consult on a strange box at the museum, the last thing he expects to find is a cure for the disease that's killing him. But nothing's that easy.

It's 1915, the world's at war, and the same magic that can keep Charlie alive is being turned into a weapon in the wrong hands.

Charlie's caught in a desperate race to survive, keep his relationship with Henry a secret, and save the world from a mad wizard who just might make the Germans look good. The *Magic Box* by Scott Thrower is available on Amazon.

Available in bookstores and at
www.losthallway.com

LOST HALLWAY
Where do lost things go?

Written by Peter G. Reynolds
Illustrated by Keith Grachow

"Hail to Canada's Dr. Seuss!
Peter G. Reynolds and Keith Grachow
have produced a charming
children's book. Bravo!"

Robert J. Sawyer
Hugo & Nebula Award-winning author

A Long Time Ago, In City-States Far Away . . .
Review of Guy Gavriel Kay's *A Brightness Long Ago* by Lisa Timpf

In his latest novel, *A Brightness Long Ago*, international best-selling author Guy Gavriel Kay revisits a world portrayed in some of his previous books, including *Sailing to Sarantium* (released in 1998) and *Lord of Emperors* (2000). *A Brightness Long Ago* is set at a time when Sarantium's influence is waning and the city itself is under siege. For the most part, *A Brightness Long Ago* focuses on events in the various city-states of Batiara, whose culture evokes Renaissance Italy.

The novel is primarily driven by the reminiscences of protagonist Guidanio Cerra. Despite his humble beginnings as a tailor's son, Guidanio has risen to a position of importance in his home city of Seressa. The novel is framed by Guidanio's musings as he thinks back on the key events of his life.

Kay presents Guidanio's narrative in first person, but as the story progresses he fleshes it out the story by providing third-person perspectives from various participants. This keeps the action moving forward, builds tension, and provides the reader with a richer understanding of events and the motivations of the various characters.

Guidanio had the good fortune of receiving an education at a prestigious school in Avegna, where he "learned to write with skill... to speak gracefully in good company and debate with clarity. To deal with weapons and the new form of accounting. To sing (with less grace, in truth), and to ride and handle horses—which became my joy in life." (p. 5)

After completing his education, Guidanio has a front row seat to some of the important events of his world through encounters with some of the great people of his time. Mercenary leaders Folco Cino and Teobaldo Monticola are two such figures. Widely recognized as the top two mercenary leaders of their era, the men exhibit a deep-seated dislike of each other. Other important figures Guidanio encounters include Antenami Sardi and Adria Ripoli, members of two of Batiara's most powerful families.

Several of the key characters in *A Brightness Long Ago* are outsiders for one reason or another. Adria Ripoli desires "more freedom than the world wished to give a woman." (p. 11) She is able, for a time, to escape the constraints of societal expectations by undertaking covert assignments on behalf of Folco Cino, and by disguising herself as a man to compete in the Bischio horse race. Jelena, a healer, believes in many powers, "in forests and rivers, overhead in the sky, deep in the earth," (p. 38) even though such beliefs are considered heretical at a time when the predominant religion is worship of the sun god Jad. Ginevra della Valle, Teobaldo Monticola's mistress, longs for the legitimization offered by marriage—not for her own interests, but to solidify future prospects for her two sons. Even Guidanio himself is an outsider, a man not of noble birth who nonetheless takes advantage of his education and his encounters with the rich and powerful to advance his position in the world. These underdog characters give the reader someone to root for as the novel progresses.

The world described in *A Brightness Long Ago* contains both an exotic strangeness, and a haunting familiarity. The novel was inspired by Kay's research into historical Italy, which accounts in part for the sense of familiarity. At the same time, the novel is set on a different world—one with two moons, unique city-states, and a culture in which worship of the sun god Jad is the prevalent religion. There are other-worldly elements as well. For example, the reader is made privy to the thoughts of the dead, an apparition appears to one of the characters, and a seeming miracle occurs in relation to a betting ticket.

Kay's latest novel is interesting for its concepts and descriptions, and its ability to build a picture of daily life in a different time and place. While there is action—assassinations, attempted coups, battles, horse races, and the like—the novel does not take the reader on a direct course from point A to point B, driving toward a specific goal. Curiosity and an affection for the characters are what draw the reader forward, as opposed to a nail-biting edge-of-the-seat plot. That doesn't mean that the story drags. Kay utilizes dialogue, the perspectives of multiple characters, and inter-woven facts about mercenary warfare and daily life to keep the reader engaged.

Kay's descriptions of the ins and outs of mercenary warfare

are of particular interest. Ideally, "the art of war in their time was to achieve one's military goals without fighting at all." (p. 308) Mercenaries could sometimes be paid to switch sides. The same army might fight for one city-state during one campaign, and then represent an erstwhile enemy the following spring. Sieges, negotiations, posturing, and subterfuge are tools of the trade just as much as as swords and cannons might be termed so.

In addition to the depiction of mercenary warfare, the philosophical musings are another of the novel's appeals. The complex relationship between choice and chance is one theme that the protagonist Guidanio Cerra reflects upon. How and why do we make choices? What is the relationship between fate and intention? Though these are Guidanio's musings, in a sense they are also questions the reader might ask themselves. This connection lends the novel a deeper resonance.

Though the events are portrayed as happening in the past and (in this case) on a different world, some of the observations seem pertinent in our own time and place. Guidanio notes that "it was interesting, I suppose it still is, how vicious men can take power and be accepted, supported by those they govern, if they bring with them a measure of peace. If granaries are full and citizens fed. If war doesn't bring starvation to the walls." (p. 6) The idea that people will tolerate much from their leaders if the economy is thriving and basic needs are taken care of rings true even today.

Kay's acknowledgements at the end of the book allude to his research into *condottieri* warfare, the city-states of Renaissance Italy, and the feud between Montefeltro and Malatesta families in fifteenth century Italy. He notes that he also gathered information about medieval medicine and the lives of Renaissance women. Perhaps because of this extensive preparation, the novel rings with authenticity. Though the events described are fictional, while immersed in the book the reader can be excused for thinking they are fact.

Years ago, I read the three books in Kay's Fionavar Tapestry, which relates the adventures of five people transported from Toronto into a world steeped in mythology where magic is real. I deeply enjoyed the series, which begins with the book *The Summer Tree*. To this day, I count the trilogy, along with certain of Andre Norton's works and Ursula Le Guin's Earthsea novels, as my all-time favorites. So whenever I've read one of Kay's subsequent works, I've done so with a secret hope that I might find the same kind of magic between the pages.

As was the case with *Sailing to Sarantium*, which I read some years ago, I found *A Brightness Long Ago* interesting enough, but not as compelling as the Fionavar works. I realize it's unrealistic and perhaps unfair of me to wish them to be. They are very different stories. *A Brightness Long Ago*, for example, doesn't have the mythological underpinnings and the fantastic elements, such as mages, that *The Summer Tree* and its companion books provided. I also found myself connecting more with the Fionavar Trilogy characters (both the Earth-based ones and the Fionavar ones) than I did with the characters in *A Brightness Long Ago*. Adria Ripoli, Guidanio Cerra, and the rest of the cast of Kay's latest book were likeable enough. I just didn't feel the same degree of empathy for them. The feud between

Teobaldo Monticola and Folco Cino got resolved toward the end of the novel, but I wasn't all that invested beyond a mild interest in how it would turn out.

I don't mean to say that I found *A Brightness Long Ago* to be without its appeal. I found myself empathizing with, and sometimes nodding in agreement with, Guidanio Cerra's thoughts, particularly his contemplation of the complex relationship between choice and chance. Like Guidanio, I have marvelled at the notion that the decision to take a different path here andare there might have sent my life down a totally different path. I also enjoyed Kay's depiction of Batiara's culture, the insights into mercenary warfare, and in particular the chapters dealing with the quirky Bischio horse race and its eccentric rules.

With fourteen novels and one book of poetry to his credit, Kay is an accomplished writer. In *A Brightness Long Ago*, Kay's experience and mastery of craft shine through in smooth-reading prose, convincing dialogue, and descriptions which immerse the reader in the events as they occur. The inter-weaving of elements inspired by Kay's research add a layer of meaning to the novel. Readers who are looking for a repeat of the Fionavar Tapestry shouldn't expect to find it here. But those who enjoy masterful prose, who like speculative fiction with a historical underlay, or who enjoyed *Sailing to Sarantium* and others of Kay's similar works will find that *A Brightness Long Ago* has much to offer.

Given: An Interview with Fantasy Author Nandi Taylor

DFS.: I'd like to talk specifics about world-building and magic systems, but could you first give some context for the discussion—a log-line or elevator pitch for *Given?*

NT: *Given* is a young adult fantasy romance about an Island princess who travels abroad to save her ailing father and her experiences with culture shock, prejudice, and shape-shifting dragons.

DFS: What makes Given different? There's a lot of fantasy out there—what is unique about yours?

NT: My aim with *Given* was to take some of the most prevalent and problematic tropes in romantic fiction and subvert them—in particular the romanticising of the possessive alpha male. That's always scary to do, as there's the risk of accidentally reinforcing the tropes you're trying to subvert, but based on early reviews it seems like I got it right. I also wanted to create a fantasy romance story that didn't skimp on the worldbuilding and magic. I've read a lot of paranormal romance, but the ones I enjoyed the most had a rich world to support the characters.

DFS: Your novel grapples with and subverts the age-old notion of love as destined or predetermined. It also confronts some of the problematic behaviour typically displayed by love interests in young adult fiction. What message would you like to send to young readers about romantic relationships?
NT: That jealousy and possessiveness are not expressions of love, only immaturity. Neither is infatuation without respect and empathy.

DFS: How do you strike a balance between the fantasy and romance elements of your novel? How did you decide which of the two genres to emphasize?
NT: I wanted both the details of the world—politics, culture, magic, food—and the emphasis on interpersonal relationships, (especially between the romantic leads) to have equal page time. I love fantasy romance, but until the recent boom in young adult fantasy books it was tough to find a book that put just as much effort into developing the fantasy world as its own character as it did into the romance plot, and I enjoy the escapism of both.

DFS: What is it about fantasy as a genre that you think audiences —particularly young adult audiences—connect with so strongly?
The world today is tougher and more stressful to navigate than ever before. With the prevalence of the internet, and more accurately the rise of social media, the haves can no longer sweep the ugly truths about our society under the rug, especially since the have-nots now have a platform of unprecedented reach from which to air them. I think a lot of us are doing our best to be

decent people, to call out and correct injustice or, at the very, very least, feeling guilty about it, and that can be exhausting. For better or worse *Marvel* movies, *Harry Potter* books or series like *Black Mirror* can take us away from the stresses of our own world for a while to worlds that are better or worse where we have no stake and can simply act as a voyeur. Note that while I think this escapism is the appeal, it's not the only function of speculative media. It's a fantastic genre for holding up a mirror to our own society while creating a filter to help us better process feelings of disillusionment, fear, and anger while also creating hope.

DFS: What were you hoping to accomplish with your world-building, and what sources did you draw on?
NT: The plan is to write a world so immersive you miss your stop on the subway. I wanted to create a fantasy in every sense of the word—an escape. But equally as important, I wanted to see my own culture reflected in a genre I've loved my whole life. My main character's Gods are based on the Yoruba pantheon of Gods, and I draw on both West African and Caribbean traditions to inform my main characters. Lastly, I needed to create a social structure that was similar to the one we live in today in order to critique existing structural racism.

DFS: Let's talk about magic systems. How is magic handled in your books? How does it work?
NT: The magic systems are tied closely to the themes of the book, as different cultures do magic in different ways. One of my princess's struggles is that she's very good at the magic of her

culture, but struggles with the magic of the empire where she goes to study. She's also heartbroken to learn that the magic of her homeland is considered primitive and even ungodly abroad.

DFS: Farah Mendlesohn distinguishes different categories of fantasy based on how the magic is encountered. In portal fantasies, like *Alice in Wonderland*, an ordinary character is brought into a magic world; in intrusion fantasies, like *Dracula*, magic intrudes into the ordinary world of the character; in immersion fantasies, like *Lord of the Rings*, the characters live in a magic "secondary world". What category is the best fit for your stories, and why did you take that narrative strategy?
NT: Given is a secondary world fantasy. My main character, Yenni, comes from a tribe that favors the Yoruba of Nigeria pre colonization, and her gods are based on Yoruba Orisha. Her romantic interest, Weysh, is from the empire of Cresh, which is loosely based on 18th century England and France.

DFS: Some people think that portal fantasy are more appropriate for younger readers—*Alice in Wonderland*, *Chronicles of Narnia*, *Harry Potter*—because they ease the reader into the magic through a character that's easier to identify with; intrusion fantasy, like *Twilight*, are arguably easier for readers for the same reason; a rich secondary world fantasy like in *Given* could be expected to be more difficult. Did you have any issues with introducing the richness of your world to readers? How did you manage exposition of the diverse fantasy elements of your world, from a planning and technical execution level?

NT: If we're taking diversity to mean the non-Western elements that made up the folklore of the world, I parcelled them out much the same way I did the Western ones—through short internal monologue or relevant dialogue. It especially helped that my main character is travelling to a new place for the first time, so that gave me lots of license to explain things without it seeming irrelevant.

Since this is a fantasy novel, a lot of the names, terms, societal norms, etc. are made up, whether they are based in African or European traditions. I'd say beta-readers are your best friends here. Sometimes I'd be so sure that I wrote out that clever explanation for why say, people cover their mouths when facing the police instead of raising their hands, but I never actually did haha.

DFS: Brandon Sanderson's first law of magics says that resolving conflicts with magic is only satisfying to the extent that the reader understands the rules of the magic. Some authors also distinguish "hard fantasy" and "soft fantasy" based on the emphasis placed on rules and limitations in their magic systems. Can you talk a bit about your thoughts on these issues in relation to the magic systems of your stories?

NT: I agree with that sentiment, and I think it's fun to give magic strict rules, write myself into a corner and try to MacGyver my way out of it with what I have. One of the conflicts Yenni faces is that she finds the new rules to Creshen magic nebulous and difficult to grasp. The magic of both cultures in the story has concrete rules and each means of performing magic has strengths and weaknesses.

DFS: There's been a call for greater diversity in the fantasy genre. How do you see your writing in this broader discussion?

NT: It's been very heartening to see the strides made in fantasy over the last decade. We're getting diverse fantasy in more ways than one, as with the rise in stories from different identities we're getting a refreshing influx of fantasy stories with varied themes and structures.

Seeing more and more fantasies featuring characters of colour gave me the confidence to shoot my shot. One of my favourite quotes to live by is from Nelson Mandela: "And as we let our own light shine, we unconsciously give other people permission to do the same." Just posting my story on Wattpad I received comments from so many readers who were excited to read a fantasy story with a black girl as the protagonist, and to see nods to their own culture. So I now see it as my responsibility to bring the black girl magic and write the best books I can featuring women of colour.

DFS: What do you think about the #ownvoices movement?

NT: I think as representation in fantasy has increased it must also evolve, and the #ownvoices movement sprung up out of that necessity. It's not enough anymore (and to be honest it never was) to have a token gay best friend, or women who exist solely to die and further the emotional devolopment of a man, or people of colour who are magical and mystical simply because they are not white. When stories are told from the perspective of the people they are about, these gaffes in representation don't happen.

DFS: I think there is a misguided perception among some literary

critics that fantasy is somehow less important than strictly realist literature. I would say that the literary genre and the fantasy genre are equally capable of banality or profundity. The fantasy genre uses different storytelling tools and conventions, but those tools can be used for examining and expressing important themes and concepts—maybe better than realist literature in some cases. Do you consider your work as covering issues of importance to the human experience? Can you talk about how you've used speculative elements and the fantasy genre to that end?

NT: Absolutely. It's a fantasy romance but it tackles some tough topics. I draw a lot on my own experiences to inform Yenni's life abroad, and the poor girl has to deal with misogyny and constant microaggressions, but it's not all bad. There's still that sense of wonder and whimsy inherent in fantasy as she explores her new world, and she makes life-long friends. So much fantasy takes on real world issues now, especially fantasy coming from marginalised authors. The notion that sci-fi and fantasy lack the sophistication of "real" literature is quite frankly antiquated and uninformed. There's simply too much critically acclaimed speculative fiction out to substantiate it.

DFS: Have you had any unexpected reactions to your stories, or any feedback that has really stood out or affected you? Do you like hearing from and communicating with readers, and is there a good way for fans to connect with you?

NT: Putting my story on *Wattpad* has been overwhelmingly positive in my experience. Feedback from readers was vital to my editorial process for the novel. But what is most delightfully surprising to me is that a paranormal romance featuring an explicitly black heroine has gained such popularity. Sad to say, I don't know how possible this would have been ten years ago. There seemed to be this unspoken rule that a black female lead, especially in romance, was not universally relatable. I'm very happy to prove that false.

I love interacting with fans and I'm all over social media: Wattpad, Instagram, and Twitter.

DFS: How do you feel a platform like Wattpad is changing the way we engage with fiction, both as writers and as readers? How did it affect the creative process for Given?

By far the greatest advantage to posting online is crowdsourcing reader feedback. Comments from Wattpadders helped me identify when parts of the story were too predictable, or maybe a joke wasn't landing the way I wanted it to, or whether a character was as sympathetic as I wanted them to be. It's like market research.

DFS: What does it mean to you to see Yenni depicted on the front cover of Given?

It's a dream come true. For decades we've been pretending to live in a post-racial society, but it wasn't until very recently, and I'm talking like five years ago, that you could have black character on the front of your fantasy book without bringing down the marketability, having it written off as "niche". It may have taken a while for me to finally get a book on shelves, but I'm happy to be publishing now when a cover like this is not only acceptable, but the expectation for a book featuring a black protagonist.

~

Nandi Taylor is a Canadian author of Caribbean descent based in Toronto. Common themes she writes about are growth, courage, and finding one's place in the world. Her debut novel *Given* received over 1 million reads online before being picked up for publication by *Wattpad Books*.

Given can be found online in stores and online at Amazon, Indigo/Chapters in Canada, Barnes and Noble in the US and Waterstones in the UK.

Craft: Alternative Dialogue Attribution
David F. Shultz

The standard dialogue tag is "said". Some people like to spice up their dialogue by using alternatives like "continued", "replied", "stated", "joked", "answered", and so on, or by adding adverbs, as in "said tersely", or "said angrily". As a matter of subjective taste, I would caution against such alternative dialogue attributions. They have their place, of course, but they are easy to overdo, and easy to do badly.

For the most part, "said" is invisible to the reader, functioning more-or-less like punctuation. The reader passes over it quickly, and it doesn't get in the way of reading. It keeps the pace quick. By contrast, synonyms like "stated" or "explained" or "answered" or "replied" add syllables and slow pacing without offering anything in return. This category of alternatives should be ruthlessly cut in edits. When you deviate from "said", you should have a good reason for doing it, because it is always a trade-off with pacing.

Verbs like "joked" or "pleaded" add shades of meaning. In many cases, these should also be avoided. They are often redundant, since it should be obvious from the surrounding context and the content of the dialogue whether something is a joke or a plea, for example, so you aren't getting anything by using these terms. They are also "telling" instead of showing—don't tell us a character joked or pleaded; show us that it is a joke or a plea.

Some dialogue tags specify the manner in which something is said, like "shouted" or "whined" or "wheezed" or "screeched". These verbs can be useful for characterizing a manner of speech, but they need to be used in moderation. If your established baseline is "said", and suddenly a character "screeches", it will feel more screechy. Conversely, if you constantly use alternatives, the reader will gloss over them, and they will have less effect. Your ability to use alternatives for effect depends on you using them sparingly.

All of this applies as well to adverbial modifiers on "said". You could write "said tersely", or you could just write terse dialogue—the terseness should be in the dialogue, so explicitly indicating that it is terse is redundant, and it is also "telling" instead of showing. You could say "said angrily" or "said wearily", or use any of a variety of emotion-laden adverbs on "said", but in all cases this will constitute "telling" instead of showing. If the reader can't tell that someone is angry or sad or happy without being explicitly told, this might indicate a problem with how the scene is written.

You can often omit attribution entirely, particularly when there are only two speakers. If you can get away with it, it's a good strategy, because it keeps the pacing quick.

Attribution can also be omitted when you have intercessory actions or intercessory narration between dialogue. If a character takes some action in the same paragraph as the dialogue, it is understood that they are the one speaking. Likewise, narration can cue the reader as to who is speaking. This can be an elegant option, but when overdone or forced it is among the clunkiest of the alternative attribution strategies, getting in the way of dialogue and substantially slowing the pacing. Intercessory actions shouldn't ever be added for the sole purpose of indicating the speaker; there should always be some other function being performed, either progressing the action, revealing information, or developing character. Intercessory actions should also be avoided if they are redundant; you shouldn't describe a character nodding if the content of their dialogue is just stating their agreement, for example.

There are genre differences to account for here. YA writing tends to have more alternative dialogue attribution; characters always seem to be screeching or joking or pleading or saying angrily, rather than just saying things. Different genres have different expectations, and it pays to have a good sense of the genre in which you are writing. The rule to "avoid alternative dialogue attribution" is relative to genre and style; the bar is different depending on what you are writing and who you are writing for.

To sum up the various strategies for alternative dialogue attribution:

- synonyms for "said" that don't offer anything more, like "stated", "replied", and "answered": cut ruthlessly
- alternatives with tonal colour, like "joked", or "pleaded": avoid—they are often either redundant or "telling" instead

of "showing"

- alternatives that specify the manner in which something is said, like "screeched" or "groaned": minimize—they are powerful tools but their power depends on being used sparingly
- adverbial modifiers on "said", like "said angrily" or "said tersely": avoid—they are often either redundant or "telling" instead of "showing"
- omitting attribution entirely: use it where it remains clear who is speaking—it speeds up pacing
- intercessory actions to indicate speaker: only use these if it is performing some narrative function(s) other than indicating speaker

Of course, there are exceptions to all of this. The most important thing is to be controlled and judicious in your use of language. Developing craft is not about mindlessly following rules; it is about understanding the underlying rationale for the "rules" so that you can use whichever techniques are most effective for your story.

Response from Y.M. Pang:

Alternative dialogue attributions aren't innately offensive. However, they distract the reader from the actual dialogue. And because dialogue attribution usually comes after the dialogue, chances are the reader has read what the characters said and imagined the tone for themselves—only to find out after the fact that the character was actually screeching, enunciating, or offering gently. Characters can also come across as cartoonish if they're shrieking and protesting all the time.

I confess, I was once on the other side of this debate. Years ago, a much younger me argued with a creative writing teacher about alternative dialogue attribution. She, like David, said not to use them. She, unlike David, did not adequately explain why not. I —the younger one—argued that numerous famous books used them; she pointed out that many of these were intended for a middle grade or teen audience, rather than an adult one.

She had a point. Alternative dialogue attributions are more accepted in middle grade novels compared to adult ones. Perhaps it's to serve as a vocabulary teaching tool. Perhaps those narratives and characters are more exaggerated, so that people bellowing or hissing does not cause a tonal shift. Or perhaps younger readers aren't as adamant about "transparent prose," "show don't tell" and other rules that writing advice articles like this one hammer into people as they grow up.

What does this all mean? I'm in agreement with David, but I'm not super insistent on this being a "rule." It's more a convention, and one small part of craftsmanship. If I meet my younger self, I'm not going to debate about dialogue attributions. Instead, I'll tell myself to work on my actual dialogue. Oh, and fix those purple prose-y descriptions.

Instead of saying, "Don't use alternative dialogue attributions," I would say, use your judgement. Read what you've written out loud. Does the alternative attribution add anything to the dialogue? Can the dialogue be rewritten to render the attribution unnecessary? Is the attribution appropriate in the context, and is it even a proper dialogue attribution (I've seen too many writers mistake "smiled" for a dialogue attribution)? Conversely, does switching to "said" make the dialogue *more* awkward?

The answers to these questions will tell you what attribution to use. Most times, I think you'll find good old reliable "said" does the job fine.

—Y.M. Pang

Y.M. Pang is a Toronto-based author whose fiction has appeared in *The Magazine of Fantasy & Science Fiction*, *Strange Horizons*, *Clarkesworld*, and many other venues. She is a Submissions Editor with *Speculative North*, and a dabbler in photography and art.

Response from Brandon Butler:

Using 'said' is safe advice, but I believe the main alternatives to using said are using no attribution at all, or intercessory action.

Most conversations involve only two characters, and after one use of 'said' kicks things off, you can usually imply the speakers for a few lines by the order in which the quotes appear. In sequential lines of unattributed dialogue, the speaker alternates, with person A speaking odd-numbered lines and person B speaking even numbered lines. This can be continued indefinitely, though 4 unattributed lines is probably a good limit before applying some other means of reminding the reader who's speaking:

"I tire of writing dialog," I said.

"It's not so bad."

"I just don't know how to identify the speakers."

"No? I wouldn't worry—watch."

Ok, so the above dialog example directly prompts further action: hey, nothing's perfect. But for me it *also* feels like a natural break from the back and forth.

Meanwhile, intercessory actions provide an entire library of possibilities before even considering the use of 'said' again, let alone an alternative. It's like blocking in theater: your characters can move around, shake heads, shrug shoulders, do anything to add color to the scene.

And just like theater or film, the point should be to use dialog when there is a need. Think about what you are trying to convey. Is there a way of doing it without dialog? Then 9 times out of 10, I find it's better to do so (unless you've made a habit of underusing dialog TOO much). If a character is simply agreeing with a statement, nodding in response or some other gesture might be preferred.

Part of the art of writing should be to have the reader infer as much as possible, without making it feel like work. Make them WANT to read between the lines and work things out themselves. Too often, dialog spells things out, robbing the reader of an opportunity to speculate on what was meant by that last passage, or what may lie ahead.

—Brandon Butler

Brandon Butler is a Nova Scotian author currently living in

Toronto. He is a former winner of the *Writers of the Future* contest, and his work is forthcoming from or has appeared in *Helios Quarterly Magazine*, *Third Flatiron Publishing* and *Bad Dream Entertainment*.

Response from Justin Dill:

While the conventional view is that "said bookisms" should be avoided (or at least used sparingly), there's a tendency to conflate such stylistic advice with "rules" that writers ought to memorize. We are taught to say no—rather than to declare, proclaim, or ejaculate no—to alternative dialogue attributions. But as with all such rules, this rule may occasionally be broken, so long as it is broken properly.

Why not use synonyms for said? Said synonyms, after all, must exist to serve some purpose. An extensive vocabulary rarely rears its head in everyday conversation; rather, it is in prose, especially prose of the artistic persuasion, that we are liberated from the constraints of the dreaded "plain language" and free to plunder the vast depths of the English language. If there is ever a time to postulate, quip, or avow, it is in our literary exploits.

The key is knowing how to use such words as tools rather than crutches. Don't have your character thunder something because your dialogue did not sufficiently convey the extent of their volume; have them thunder something because you've been using meteorological terms in association with them to communicate something about their character—say, their stormy disposition. Don't use "exclaimed" because you want to cut down on instances of the word "said" in your manuscript; use it because another character "claimed" something in the previous line and you enjoy a bit of harmless wordplay (and consider having the next character "disclaim" their dialogue). Don't use "quod" as a dialogue attribution because you learned it in English class and were mesmerized by the sound of it; use it because you're evoking a very particular old-fashioned narrative voice to fit the atmosphere of your historical novel.

If "said" is invisible, it doesn't allow any opportunity for uniqueness. If all writers adhere to the same formula (in this case, the same method of dialogue attribution), that's one less way in which writers can distinguish their narrative voices from one another. It's common to think of dialogue attributions as part of the dialogue, as a cheap way to convey emotion that should have been conveyed in the character's words themselves. But dialogue attribution is equally part of the narration, contributing to that nebulous concept we refer to as tone. And what of pacing? If dialogue attributions other than said aren't invisible, they require more brain power to process and cause the reader to slow down and read a dialogue-heavy section of your narrative a little more slowly, where otherwise their eyes might have swiftly glazed over it.

As always, it's important to know the downsides to breaking any rule. Use too many words that require heavy brain power to process, and you risk overwhelming the reader. Convey too much emotion in dialogue attributions, and you risk spoon-feeding emotions to your reader rather than genuinely evoking emotions. Have your characters boom, bellow, and boisterously bark things too frequently, and those words lose their meaning. Alternative dialogue attributions—like adverbial modifiers and intercessory actions—are a part of any good writer's toolbox. It's our job as writers to learn when and how to use those tools effectively.

—Justin Dill

Justin Dill is a Toronto-based writer of young adult fiction, a grammar enthusiast, and a horror movie buff. You can enlist his editorial services at royaleditorial.com. He also co-hosts the podcast *Story from Scratch* and releases music under the name *Bloo Burds*.

Exercise: Seven Nuns in an Elevator
David F. Shultz

Often, writers will use superficial features to distinguish characters. This can be seen, for example, in some high fantasy, where writers will insert a token elf with a bow, or a token dwarf with an axe. More generally, by ascribing different professions, races, ages, or physical appearances, writers create characters that can be distinguished superficially, but not necessarily with any meaningful depth.

The "Seven Nuns in an Elevator" exercise forces writers to avoid these superficial strategies. The goal is to write a scene with seven nuns stuck in an elevator. The nuns share the same gender, religion, clothing, and station in life; if they are going to be distinguished, it must be through some other means, such as how their personalities exhibit through dialogue and action.

They don't have to be nuns trapped in an elevator. You could pick some science fiction or fantasy scenario that provides similar constraints: a relatively simple setting in which the characters are trapped, and a class of person that is relatively homogenous as it concerns clothing, ideology, and social function. You could have seven knights trapped in a cave, for example, or seven starship marines on a crashed shuttle.

Your task is simple: write a scene with seven of these characters, such that by the end of the scene, the reader has a sense of the different characters. Come up with different personalities for each of them, and present that through various means of characterization.

Suggested scenarios/prompts:

- Seven knights trapped in a dragon's cave
- Seven AI scout drones in an asteroid field
- Seven starship marines on a crashed shuttle
- Seven alien worms stuck in a rover's sample collector

Toronto author Martin Munks has provided an example science fiction execution of the "Seven Nuns" exercise, called "Nautical Unit Ninety-Six":

Nautical Unit Ninety-Six
by Martin Munks

"What do you mean it's broke?" asked Nancy.

"You mean broken," corrected Angelica.

"I know what I said."

Cherry shone a maglite into an open panel beside the elevator door, illuminating wisps of smoke among the circuitry. "Looks like a severed rangaloon cable. Could fix it if I had a calico-max andulator, or at least some brachial Y-funnels. But my toolkit is topside."

"We're as good as dead," whispered Juliet. "I always imagined the ocean would get me. Drowning, you know? Or mangled in a car accident. Not trapped in an elevator until we run out of air and asphyxiate."

The seven members of Nautical Unit Ninety-Six began speaking all at once, voices echoing off of the metal walls.

"Calm down," said Tess, holding out an open palm. The cramped space quieted immediately. "Ideas. Go."

Hannah slowly raised her hand. "Um, maybe if we break through, uh, well, no. Or if we bang that wrench against the, uh, no that won't work either. Sorry." Her hand went down.

Gloria knelt, folding her gloved fingers together. "Dear Zenex, if you're listening, please show your infinite mercy and spare us."

"If your stupid God existed, he would of helped us already."

"Would have."

"I know what I said. And wait, how did you even—"

"People! Let's focus. Comms?"

"None. The ship's zigzagonal array doesn't penetrate this deep, not without a beam-wrangler."

"Maybe if we, if we use our, um, no. No, nevermind. Forget it everyone, sorry."

"Dehydration? That's another way to go. If it's not airtight in here, we'll run out of water pretty soon."

"If only I had a smartwave tantalizer! I could use it to solder the severed rangaloon cables."

"Oh! Uh, I might, uh, have one in my pack for, well, no, not for anything really. But I have one! I think."

"Good thinking. Will it work?"

"Yes, once I've redazzled the power circuits."

"Then go. Get working."

"Zenex be praised!"

"Oh no, this sudden excitement is making me dizzy. Stroke maybe? Or a heart attack, that seems more likely."

"There. Rangaloon cables reintegrated. Here goes nothing."

The elevator lurched to a start, moving up toward the surface. Sighs all around.

"Good work team! Well done."

"You know, I thought for sure we was gonna be trapped for days."

"We're gonna be trapped for days."

"I know what I said."

Comments by David F. Shultz:

In "Nautical Unit Ninety-Six", Martin effectively uses alternative dialogue attribution for characterization. Dialogue tags like "whispered" and "corrected" help establish character early on. Angelica is established as the sort of person to correct people, so we recognize her later corrective lines, even when they are unattributed. Juliet's whisper is connected to the pessimism in her dialogue, and she is established as a kind of Eeyore character. We recognize her later pessimistic lines, though unattributed, and probably hear them in the same voice.

Martin uses intercessory action to indicate speaker and establish character. Hannah is tentative and reserved, expressed by slowly raising her hand to speak. Gloria is devoutly religious, expressed by kneeling and folding hands together to pray.

Towards the end, Martin presents a series of dialogue quotes without any attribution, intercessory action, or narration of any kind. Because of the earlier characterization, we know to whom each of these lines of dialogue belongs.

About the Contributors

Nathan Batchelor
Author, "Tokyo Burning"
Nathan grew up in Appalachian Alabama under the tutelage of a bootlegger Grandma. He lives in and writes fiction from Columbus, Ohio. He graduated with a degree in biology from Ohio State University. You can find him on twitter @NateBatchelor

Gregg Chamberlain
Author, "It's Always Ice Time in the D.H.L."
Gregg Chamberlain is a community newspaper reporter, five decades in the trade, living in rural Ontario, with his missus, Anne, and their two cats, who allow the humans to believe they are in charge. He looks forward to retirement so he can devote more time to his fiction work, which is how he has fun. He has more than five dozen short-fiction credits in various anthologies and venues like *Daily Science Fiction, Abyss & Apex, Mythic, Nothing Sacred, Weirdbook,* and other magazines.

Evan Dicken
Author, "Citizen of the Galaxy"
By day, Evan Dicken studies old Japanese maps and crunches data for all manner of fascinating medical experiments at the Ohio State University. By night, he does neither of these things. His fiction has most recently appeared in: *Analog, Cossmass Infinities, Strange Horizons,* and he has stories forthcoming from publishers such as *Black Library* and *Beneath Ceaseless Skies.* Please feel free to visit him at evandicken.com.

Matthew Donahue

Author, "Memories White"

Matthew Donahue is a Canadian speculative fiction writer, award-winning short film producer and videographer born in Ottawa, currently based in Toronto. You can find him on Twitter here: @Monopolisticaly

A. B. Eyers

Author, "Kariku's Ocean"

A. B. Eyers lives in a small off-grid cabin in northern Canada, which she shares with one husband and one large Newfoundland dog, as well as the occasional (and quickly evicted) pine marten. Since completing her bachelor's degree in Creative Writing she divides her time between summer construction work and winter travels through the secluded wilderness. Her hobbies include snowshoeing, juggling, baking and tuba playing.

Joshua Grasso

Author, "The Alchemy of Curses"

Joshua Grasso is a professor of English at a small university in Oklahoma, where he teaches classes in British and World Literature (the older, the better!). In-between teaching and grading, he has written numerous articles on literature, a few indie novels, and a handful of fantasy and science-fictions stories.

Diane Callahan

Author, "He Sold What He Had Left"

Diane Callahan strives to capture her sliver of the universe through writing fiction, nonfiction, and poetry. As a developmental editor and ghostplotter, she spends her days shaping stories. Her YouTube channel, Quotidian Writer, provides practical tips for aspiring authors. You can read her work in *Translunar Travelers Lounge, Short Édition, Riddled with Arrows, Rust+Moth,* and *The Sunlight Press,* among others.

Christina Ladd
Author, "Mona Luna"
Christina Ladd is a writer, editor, and librarian living in Boston. She will eventually die crushed under a pile of books, but until then, she survives on tea and a truly staggering amount of carbs.

Lynne M MacLean
Author, "Grass Whisperer"
Lynne M MacLean has had short fiction and poetry published in *On Spec Magazine, Room Magazine, PodCastle, Stupefying Stories, Horrific History: An Anthology of Historical Horror*, and *Tesseracts Fifteen: A Case of Quite Curious Tales*, among others. She currently works as a community health research consultant and writer in Ottawa, Ontario, Canada, and previously, as a mental health practitioner in Canada's prairies and remote Northwest Territories. She is married, and the mother of two young adults, plus one cat. None of them read her writing, although the cat can be bribed occasionally. Lynne can be found at:
www.LynneMMacLean.com and @LynneMacLean2

Lisa Timpf
Author, "A Long Time Ago, In City-States Far Away . . ."
Lisa Timpf is a retired HR and communications professional who lives in Simcoe, Ontario. Her speculative poetry, fiction, and creative non-fiction has appeared in a variety of venues, including *New Myths, The Future Fire, Star*Line, Liminality*, and *Eye to the Telescope*. You can find out more about Lisa's writing at http://lisatimpf.blogspot.com/.